M

MW01136353

Wendy the Wedding Planner Cozy Mystery

Cindy Bell

ISBN-13: 978-1500172596

ISBN-10: 1500172596

More Cozy Mysteries by Cindy Bell

Dune House Cozy Mystery Series

Seaside Secrets

Heavenly Highland Inn Cozy Mystery Series

Murdering the Roses

Dead in the Daisies

Killing the Carnations

Drowning the Daffodils

Suffocating the Sunflowers

Bekki the Beautician Cozy Mystery Series

Hairspray and Homicide

A Dyed Blonde and a Dead Body

Mascara and Murder

Pageant and Poison

Conditioner and a Corpse

Mistletoe, Makeup and Murder

Hairpin, Hair Dryer and Homicide

Blush, a Bride and a Body

Shampoo and a Stiff

Cosmetics, a Cruise and a Killer

Table of Contents

Chapter One

The scent of the sea lingered in the air as Wendy drew a deep breath. The sound of the water crashing against the sand was her morning greeting. She loved her early morning walks along the beach in Oceanside California. It was a popular resort area so there were always a few people on the beach, but Wendy would take her walk just after sunrise when there weren't many people awake. She enjoyed the quiet, and the cool sand beneath her bare toes. As Wendy looked up at the myriad of colors sprawled across the sky she felt a renewed sense of gratitude for the way her life was unfolding. At twenty-eight she had a promising career as an assistant to one of the most well-known wedding planners in all of California, Camilla Blue. Camilla had taken Wendy under her wing when she was inspired by some of the sample wedding plans that Wendy had put together in place of a resume.

Wendy was a romantic at heart, she believed that the perfect moments that some people claimed were only found in movies could be carefully crafted into reality given the right setting, and the will to make it happen. As a result her ideas for weddings were always very well thought out and took into account every tiny aspect that even the most attentive bride might overlook. She adored being part of the best moment of many people's lives.

Wendy stepped through the double glass doors that led from a small, beach-facing patio into the quaint one bedroom condo she shared with her boyfriend. It was decorated with cool blues and sea foam greens as well as some pictures of some of the weddings she had organized. Her living room had a Victorian style to it with plenty of lace and plush, comfortable furniture with wooden accents. She padded quietly into the kitchen, not wanting to wake Aaron before it was time for his alarm to go off. He worked at a beach bar as a very popular bartender and he kept late hours as a result.

Her kitchen wasn't too large, but everything was within reach, which she liked. She started brewing coffee and then tip-toed into the bedroom she shared with Aaron. He had moved in a few weeks ago though he had wanted to move in much sooner. Wendy had been hoping that he would propose to her before they lived together, but when he was forced out of his apartment due to an issue with the lease, she had seen no reason not to allow him to move in. Now that they were seeing each other every day Wendy had begun to sense a distance growing between them. It made her uneasy, but she also knew that it was tourist season, he was busy and so was she.

She walked to the bedroom and stood in the doorway. She gazed at Aaron sprawled across their queen sized bed. He was bronze, there was no other way to describe him. From head to toe, it looked as if he had been glazed by the sun. He kept his body toned and lean as it helped with his tips. His blonde hair was bleached on occasion and kept long to give him that surfer look that his customers enjoyed. Though his eyes were closed in slumber Wendy knew that those pale lashes hid spheres of the clearest blue she had ever looked into. Aaron was an extremely attractive man, and Wendy felt very lucky to be with him.

She wasn't exactly a ravishing beauty, at least not in her own estimation. When you worked around women who were striving to look their very best for their wedding, it was hard to see yourself as beautiful in comparison. Her strawberry blonde curls were more strawberry than blonde and layered in a messy cut that ended just below her ears. Her heart-shaped face and deep-set, dark green eyes gave her a pixieish look that she could appreciate at times. She had a naturally slender frame, but wasn't very muscular. Her skin, despite living at the beach, insisted on being just shy of pale. She was average height, and did her best to accentuate her features with a mild amount of make-up.

Aaron snorted in his sleep and groaned as he rolled over on the bed. Wendy thought about waking him, to have a little chat before she headed off to work, but she knew he needed his rest. Instead, she changed for the day and headed off to work with Camilla already texting her. Wendy ignored the texts as she was going to be at the office within minutes. Camilla treated her less like an assistant and more like a personal servant, but Wendy didn't mind as she was grateful for the opportunity and looked forward to learning and experiencing as much as she could.

Wendy drove a small, gold SUV, she thought the color was a little obnoxious but she got a deal on it so she was willing to tolerate it. She needed a larger vehicle to cart around all of the last minute equipment and requests for weddings. Once she had to get a pair of doves to a wedding in under ten minutes, but the latch on the cage had not been closed all the way, and the birds ended up flying all over her car as she drove to the wedding. The upholstery had not been the same since. Still, Wendy had a lot of memories in the car, of other people's weddings. Not hers. But hopefully that would be changing soon. Aaron's recent change in behavior might mean he was planning an elaborate proposal. Just the thought of it made Wendy's heart speed up with excitement. Planning weddings for other people was wonderful, but the chance to plan her own would be amazing. As she pulled into the parking lot of the high rise office building that Camilla's office was located in, Wendy took a deep breath and prepared herself for what she might face when she went inside. Camilla had two moods, elated and angry. She never really seemed to settle in-between. With the amount of texts she had already fired off to Wendy, she was guessing that today was an angry day.

Camilla's office was sprawling and took up one quarter of the bottom floor of the large building. She had it decorated with shimmering chandeliers, luxurious draperies, and marble floors. There were black and white photographs of weddings she had planned covering all the walls from floor to ceiling. Walking through the large, glass door reminded Wendy of stepping into the throne room of a palace. Perched in her high-backed chair, Camilla certainly appeared to be a queen. Her glossy blonde hair was always falling at the perfect angle. Her make-up was perfectly applied, and accentuated her high-cheekbones, bold brown eyes, and full lips. She had a very youthful look about her despite being well into her forties, a secret that very few were privy to.

"Morning, Camilla," Wendy said brightly as she stepped further into the office.

"Oh, Wendy," she cleared her throat and sat up straight in her chair. Wendy stopped short at the tone in Camilla's voice. It was not one that she expected to hear. "Didn't you get my texts?"

"Is something wrong?" Wendy asked with concern. "Didn't the flowers get delivered for the Baker's dawn wedding?"

"Oh yes, they were delivered," Camilla nodded and then sighed as she laid her hands on the broad desk in front of her. "Wendy, please, take a seat."

Wendy didn't want to take a seat, but she reluctantly pulled out a wooden cushioned chair and sat down on it. Her heartbeat had quickened. She wasn't sure what to expect, but Camilla's pinched expression made her feel as if something terrible had happened.

"Wendy, you know, you've been just a wonderful assistant," Camilla said coolly.

Wendy smiled at the compliment, but her smile faded as the words sunk in.

"What do you mean, have been?" she asked in a shaky voice. "Camilla? Did I do something wrong?"

"No, of course not," Camilla insisted and shook her head. "You've helped me so much. You even brought that con artist Giuseppe Michaels to my attention, and trust me, I will be handling that situation. Unfortunately though, I've had a favor asked of me and it's from people who are like family to me."

"I don't understand," Wendy said in a murmur. "Are you firing me?"

"Firing is such an ugly word," Camilla said and then clucked her tongue lightly. "But yes," she finally finished bluntly. "My best friend's daughter needs a job, and so she gets yours," she shrugged. "It's not personal, I can assure you."

All of the air seemed to leave the room, and Wendy's lungs at once. Time froze, and Wendy couldn't begin to process the words she had just heard. Of all the things she had expected from her day, being fired was not one of them.

"Is this some kind of joke?" Wendy asked as she stared across the desk at Camilla. The high ceilings of her office allowed her to position perfect lighting above her head. She looked a bit like an angel, but Wendy did not see her that way at the moment.

"No, I'm not joking," Camilla said sternly and narrowed her eyes. "Is there something that makes you think I am?"

"Well, I," Wendy stared hard at her own hands for a long moment. She was not normally confrontational, but she had also never dealt with this kind of situation. "I helped you build this business, Camilla," Wendy breathed out. "I gave ten new weddings to you, I suggested the dawn ceremonies and..."

"Really?" Camilla asked and tilted her head slightly to the side. "Are you trying to say that I owe you something, Wendy? Perhaps you are forgetting that you are nothing more than my assistant. Yes, you did a good job. But very close friends come first. I'm sure you can understand that," she added.

Wendy's mouth dropped open as she searched for the best way to express the betrayal she was feeling. She had never expected to be let go. She expected she might even take over the business for Camilla in the future.

"Oh honey, please don't make a scene," Camilla requested and pressed a button on her telephone. "Marcia, can you come in here please?" she asked.

Wendy was familiar with this move. Camilla always called Marcia into the room when she was meeting with a less than happy client who she thought might lose their temper or end up in tears. It was always better to have a distraction. As Marcia stepped into the large office, Wendy stood up from her chair.

"I can't believe you're doing this to me, Camilla," Wendy said with tears in her eyes. "I've been nothing but loyal to you."

"And I hope that you will remember our time together fondly, as I will," Camilla replied and folded her hands on the desk in front of her as she looked up at Wendy. "Like I said it's not personal."

"But it is personal," Wendy argued, her voice raising a few octaves. "I have worked days, nights, weekends, holidays, I have done anything that you've asked of me. How could you possibly just decide to get rid of me? I don't see how that isn't personal!"

"Well, that's why you won't get far in this business," Camilla replied with ice in her tone. "The wedding business isn't about friendships, Wendy, it's about having the right clients. I can hire a million assistants, and eventually they could do their job as well as you. I'm sorry if you mistook my generous nature with you to mean that I depended on you for my success."

Wendy lowered her eyes. She blinked back her tears. She felt humiliated as Marcia stood hesitantly by the door. Wendy had handpicked Marcia to be Camilla's receptionist. She had pored over hundreds of applications and was certain that Marcia would be the perfect fit. She had been right of course.

"I can't believe this," she whispered to herself. She shook her head as she turned and began walking out of the office.

"Wendy," Camilla called out just as Wendy reached the door. Wendy turned back, expecting her to break into a laugh and claim it was all a prank, but Camilla had her hand outstretched. "I'll need your cell phone. It's on the company's plan, remember?"

Wendy reached into her small purse and pulled out her cell phone. She held onto it for a long moment. It had the contact numbers of all their clients past and present. It was her only connection to the job she had worked so hard to succeed in.

"Morning, Aunt Camilla," a cheerful voice called out. Wendy looked up in time to see a long-legged brunette walking through the door. She could have given any model a run for her money. Her figure was perfect, and not a single hair was out of place, despite the full and bouncing curls.

"Morning, Ronnie," Camilla replied with a slight sigh. "I'm sorry, I thought I would be done with this before you arrived."

"Done with this?" Wendy repeated, still in shock. She looked back at Ronnie, and held the phone out to her. "I guess this is yours now."

Ronnie took the phone hesitantly. Her eyes as brown and bold as her aunt's, but not as hardened. Wendy could detect some sympathy in them but she didn't stick around long enough to find out why. With a shake of her head she marched past Marcia and out of the office. She found herself walking straight to her car. She paused beside it and willed herself not to cry as she pushed the button on the remote to unlock the doors. The parking lot was scattered with people and she didn't want them noticing how upset she was. As she climbed into her car she sniffled and realized she couldn't even call Aaron because she no longer had a cell phone. She closed her eyes and tried to keep from melting down. So, she had been fired. It happened to thousands of people every day for far worse reasons.

Wendy started the car and began driving back to her condo. She was fighting back tears the entire time. When she opened the door to the condo she hoped that Aaron would be awake, that he would open his arms to her, and that he would kiss away every hurt feeling she had. He was awake, but his arms were occupied, carrying two packed suitcases. Wendy stared at those suitcases like they were two weapons pointed right at her.

"Aaron?" Wendy asked, though she could barely get his entire name out, the breath was stolen from her lungs.

"Wendy," he cringed, and it was evident that he hadn't expected her to be home from work. "I'm sorry, I just..."

"Are you leaving me?" Wendy asked, her eyes so wide that they burned. "You can't be serious!"

"Look Wendy, I know that you want a whole lot more than I can offer right now, and that's why I think it would be a good idea to end this now," he said as calmly as he could. His hands tightened on the handles of his suitcases.

"Wow," Wendy muttered to herself and finally the tears that she had been holding back began to fall. "I guess you really don't want to marry me."

"I'm just not ready for that," he said apologetically. "I know that you're quite traditional, and well, I didn't want to take advantage of you."

"But you already have," Wendy pointed out. "You know I didn't expect us to get married until you were ready. Did you just string me along so you would have a place to stay?" she growled. The nice, gentle Wendy was long gone. Her morning had gone from peaceful to chaos in a matter of hours and she was not willing to let things fall apart, not without a fight.

"Wendy, it wasn't like that," he insisted and shook his head, his blonde hair tumbling across his features in a way that used to be adorable to Wendy, but now just made her angry.

"Sure it was," she spat out and threw her purse down on the floor. "First Camilla takes all of my good ideas and then fires me, now, you spend months in my home until what, you got a better offer? You saved up enough money to get a place of your own?"

"Wendy," he sighed. "I know this isn't easy to hear, but it's what has to happen. I don't want marriage, I don't want kids, I like my life the way it is."

"Sure you do, with all those beautiful tourists in bikinis throwing themselves at you," Wendy laughed out loud and looked up at the ceiling as she shook her head. "I can't believe I didn't see all of this coming. I must be the stupidest person on the planet!"

"Wendy, it doesn't have to be like this," he murmured and set down his suitcases. When he reached out to her she looked back at him with fury in her eyes.

"Out," she said flatly. "Get out of here, and make sure you have everything with you. I don't want to ever see you again."

She could see a flicker of hurt in his features, and that only made her angrier. She didn't think he had a right to be hurt. She was heartbroken, her entire life had just been ripped out from under her. As he walked past her she felt her heart drop. A part of her was hoping he would turn back and admit he made a mistake. But he didn't. He just closed the door behind him. Wendy stood in her living room, alone, jobless.

She closed her eyes and fresh tears began to stream down her cheeks. She was certain that all of this had to be some kind of cosmic joke. She walked through the condo and out through the back doors that led onto the beach. She breathed in the mid-morning air. It was the same sand she had been standing in just hours before, but now it was hot. It burned the soles of her feet. She shivered and turned away from the crash and retreat of the water against the shore. She had no way to stop the tides from changing. She could only pick up what pieces remained and see if she could salvage something.

Wendy's life had been fairly average growing up, with two well-meaning parents and no siblings. She had kept to herself and read many books. But when she hit her teenage years she became addicted to romance, in movies, in books, in poetry, wherever she could find it. Unfortunately, high school boys were not the best resource for genuine romance so she hadn't dated much.

Aaron had come into her life by what she thought was a fateful accident. They had literally tripped over each other on the beach, as he was sprawled out on his surfboard in the sand getting a tan, and she was jogging beside the waves. It was a sunny morning and she had closed her eyes against the glare. She didn't see Aaron there until she tripped right over his outstretched legs. Part of her suspected that he might have tripped her on purpose. Either way, she ended up in his arms, gazing into his eyes, and she could have sworn she heard violins playing in the distance. But all of that had been a lie, obviously, because whatever romance she thought she had found had all been in her mind.

Aaron didn't feel that way about her, or he wouldn't have been able to walk away. The hardest part was facing the truth, that she didn't really feel that way about him either. She had wanted to, just because she wanted her romance, but she could now acknowledge that it was never genuine.

When she returned to the condo alone, she knew that she had two choices. She could collapse in grief, wallow in the bottom of a carton of ice-cream, and believe that her life was over. Or she could stand up and make some changes. She was trying to see what was happening to her as a new beginning, instead of an ending. It didn't make the betrayal hurt any less. First, she felt she needed to do a good cleansing.

She spent the afternoon sorting through photos of Aaron and tossing them in the trash. She came across some of Camilla as well. When she saw her perfect smile, she got angry again. She had trusted the woman, believed in her, supported her through every crisis that her company ever had. She pulled a pair of scissors out of her kitchen drawer and cut the pictures into tiny little pieces. Then she tossed them in the garbage. She had tears biting at her eyes, but she refused to let them fall. Even though things had ended so roughly with Camilla that didn't change the fact that she had learned a lot from the woman. She had honed her skills. She was now familiar enough with the business to open a wedding planning business herself. Why shouldn't she?

"I could do it," she said to herself, her mind beginning to race with the possibilities.

She smiled a little at that idea. She began to feel her positive nature returning. Maybe Camilla firing her had opened a door for her. Maybe she could be her own boss, and start something wonderful. The thought grew and grew in her mind. She soon began researching and putting together ideas for her own business. She did her best to ignore the pangs of hurt over Aaron. As her emotions had settled, she had to admit that he was right. She had been trying to force a romance between them that was never going to happen. She wanted him to be her prince charming when he was nothing more than a surfer boy who had never grown up.

Chapter Two

When Wendy woke up the next morning, she was more determined than ever to land on her feet. She wasn't going to let Camilla or Aaron knock her down. She had contacts of her own, clients she had brought in herself, and one was due to be married in a week. Camilla never would have got them as clients if it wasn't for Wendy and the bride having a mutual friend who recommended Wendy. She had a meeting planned with the couple that morning at a beachside hotel where they were holding their reception. Brenda and John were a sweet couple who were marrying later in life. Brenda had never been married before, but John had been married twice. Wendy had expected him to be reluctant about a big wedding, but he had announced at their first meeting that he wanted their wedding to be a celebration of finally getting it right.

She didn't have time to pick up a new cell phone before she headed to the meeting, which made her feel a little naked, but it was actually a little liberating for people not to be able to contact her. When she arrived at the beachside resort to meet with Brenda and John the couple was already seated at a table with a window overlooking the beach. Everything in the restaurant was crisp and white. It gave the whole place a fresh feeling. As she walked towards the couple Brenda looked up at her with a grim frown. Only then did Wendy notice a third person sitting at their table, as she had been half-hidden by one of the supporting pillars in the restaurant.

"Camilla, what are you doing here?" Wendy asked with disdain as she walked up to the table.

John shifted uncomfortably in his chair, and Brenda sniffled.

"Camilla said you couldn't work with us anymore," Brenda said with tears in her eyes. Brenda was very meticulous about her wedding and she and Wendy had gone over it with a fine tooth comb.

"I am perfectly able to work with you, Brenda," Wendy assured her as Camilla turned to look at her with her damning, dark eyes.

"The Bartholomews are my clients," Camilla

said grimly. "You can't steal them from me."

"They're actually my clients," Wendy argued, her voice more insistent than Camilla's. "I brought them in from a personal referral, and they never signed an agreement with you. They would never have come to your company if Brenda and I didn't have a mutual friend."

Brenda's soon to be husband, John, looked at the two women warily.

"Maybe we should let you two discuss this," he said as he took his fiancée's hand and led her away from the table. Camilla stood up from the chair she had been sitting on and glowered at Wendy.

"You have some nerve thinking you can just steal my clients!" Camilla nearly shouted, drawing the attention of the wait staff and other patrons in the restaurant.

"They're not your clients," Wendy hissed in return. "I am the one that has all their plans, I am the one that booked everything for them. You have no clue what Brenda wants, and I know everything about the wedding. Would you really risk ruining a couple's wedding just to be petty?"

Wendy demanded as she searched Camilla's eyes with increased fury.

"I'm not the one being petty here," Camilla snapped back and took a threatening step closer to Wendy. "You can't just walk in here and steal my business!"

"You are being petty. I'm a great wedding planner, it took you firing me to make me realize that. I don't need you, or your name, all I need are my skills, which you no longer have. So, if you'll excuse me, I'm trying to have a meeting with my clients."

"I'll never let you get away with this," Camilla warned her with a sharp edge to her voice. "You will not work in this town again!"

"I'm not afraid of you, Camilla," Wendy growled back, feeling her determination grow even stronger. "Anything you try to do to me, I'll make sure you pay for it."

Camilla stopped and looked back over her shoulder. She met Wendy's eyes directly and the heat that sparked between the two women was so intense that one of the waiters stepped up between them.

"I'm afraid I'm going to have to ask you to leave," he said calmly to Camilla.

"Me?" Camilla laughed shortly at that. "You're throwing out the wrong person. After all, she's the one that's threatening me!"

"Oh, it's not a threat, Camilla," Wendy heard herself say without thinking her words through. "It's a promise!" Wendy's temper had gotten away from her.

"We'll see about that," Camilla sneered. She turned and walked out of the restaurant.

"Are you okay?" the waiter asked as he looked over at Wendy.

"Yes," Wendy nodded and took a deep breath. "I'm sorry for causing a scene."

"Don't be," the waiter rolled his eyes which were nearly hidden beneath thick, black rimmed glasses. "I've seen that woman around enough to know she needs to be knocked down a few notches."

Wendy raised her eyebrow at that. She had never really heard anyone speak openly against Camilla as she had such a powerful influence in the wedding industry that everyone seemed to go out of their way to be kind and accommodating to her. She nodded with a slight smile to the waiter and then walked over to Brenda and John who were huddled by the bathrooms.

"I'm so sorry, Wendy, I didn't know what to say to her," Brenda gushed and rubbed her hands together nervously.

"No, I'm sorry," Wendy said firmly as she looked from John's concerned expression to the tears still building in Brenda's eyes. "You shouldn't have to deal with any of this when you're preparing for your perfect day. Don't let this disrupt any of your enjoyment, okay?" she smiled warmly at Brenda.

"Okay," Brenda sighed with relief and abruptly hugged Wendy. "I don't know what I would do without you."

Wendy smiled as she hugged Brenda back. Even though they had only known each other for a short time, Wendy was used to this kind of outpouring of affection. A woman put her complete trust in her wedding planner. It was a special kind of bond, and though it tended to fade after the wedding, until the big day it grew very quickly.

"Now, about the cake?" Wendy asked as she pulled away from Brenda. "I know your choices are limited because John is allergic to nuts."

"Deathly allergic!" John exclaimed.

"Have you managed to agree on a flavor," she asked as they walked back towards a table.

"We haven't really discussed it," John sighed as he sat down with them. "But I would like it to be pure chocolate."

"And I want vanilla," Brenda said firmly.

"Vanilla?" John scrunched up his nose. "What is the point of eating cake if it's vanilla?"

"Well, I think I found the perfect cake for you," Wendy grinned as she looked between the two. "It's a marble cake blended with vanilla and chocolate, and we can even make one side of the cake more chocolate and the other more vanilla. How does that sound?" she suggested.

"I don't know," Brenda hesitated.

"It'll be a great way to represent the two of you blending your lives together," Wendy pointed out.

"That's true," Brenda began to smile and

then nodded. "It sounds good, what do you think, John?" she asked as she looked over at him.

"As long as there are no nuts," he laughed.

As Wendy guided them through the final touches to their wedding plans she did her best to smooth over any disagreement that erupted between them. That was one thing that was sure to ruin a wedding. The planning shouldn't be stressful, or it might sour the big day itself. By the time they had finished with the meeting they had finalized their cake, the tablecloths, and a song for their first dance together as a married couple.

"All right, we have a little over a week," Wendy said as she looked at the two of them. "Don't worry, everything is going to be perfect. Make sure the two of you are taking a little time to be together, without any wedding talk, okay?"

"That would be great," John said playfully, and Brenda nodded with a sheepish smile.

"I guess it has been taking over our lives a little," she admitted.

"That's my job," Wendy assured them. "Your

job is to take a few moments each day to remember exactly how and why you fell in love, okay? Because the most important part of a wedding, is the love that you bring to it."

As Wendy stood up from the table, John and Brenda were already gazing lovingly at each other. Wendy felt a slight pang of hurt as it reminded her of Aaron, but she pushed it down. She never let her personal affairs interfere with a wedding.

***

When Wendy left the couple she went to speak to the resort staff to make sure everything was arranged for the wedding, and that Camilla hadn't thrown any wrenches into their plans. She stopped by the florist on the way home to confirm the order of pink roses, and then headed back to her condo. She completely forgot that she needed to get a cell phone. She was lost in her visualization of the Bartholomews' wedding as she went to unlock the door of her condo. She found it was already open. Her heart jumped.

Was it Aaron?

When she opened the door all the way she found that it was Aaron, but not in the way that she hoped.

"I've been trying to call you," he said with annoyance as he picked up a box he had been filling with the things he had left behind. "I tried to come when you weren't here, sorry."

"Sorry, for sneaking into my home, or breaking my heart?" Wendy challenged as she studied him.

"I don't know, both," Aaron shrugged and brushed his blonde hair away from his eyes. "This doesn't need to be painful."

"Not for you," Wendy agreed. "Just take your stuff and go," she ordered him, her blood beginning to boil.

"Don't be like that, Wendy," he murmured and put his box down. "I thought we could maybe, say goodbye, in a nicer way."

"Are you insane?" Wendy asked with wide eyes. She placed her hands on her hips and glared at him. "I think you should leave."

"All right, all right," Aaron nodded and stared at her for a long moment before picking up his box again. Wendy's heart was racing. She longed for the idea of marrying him so much that she nearly gave in. But as he walked past her with a cold expression on his face, she knew that he never really cared for her the way she thought.

***

It was hard for her to stay focused on wedding details when her mind kept drifting back to Camilla, and Aaron. Finally, she took a break and went for an evening walk along the beach. She loved the fact that she could step outside and straight onto the beach. The sand between her toes was always soothing to her, even with everything that was going on at the moment.

As Wendy paused for a moment to dip her toe in the water she noticed flashing lights far down the beach. From the distance she guessed it was near the resort area. Her stomach fluttered as she wondered what tragedy might have unfolded. It always saddened her when someone was enjoying a vacation or celebration and ended up injured or worse. She watched the glimmering lights for a few minutes before returning to her condo.

Wendy sighed and tried to focus on the wedding details again. She reminded herself that this was for Brenda and John, two people in love, and ready to start their lives together. She stayed up for another few hours adding details and changing plans, before finally collapsing into bed. It took her a little while to fall asleep. She shed a few tears at the emptiness of the bed, and the coldness in Aaron's eyes. She shed a few more for losing her mentor, and then finally she fell into an exhausted slumber.

Chapter Three

Wendy barely had her eyes open when she heard an insistent pounding on her door. She had hoped to wake up to a much brighter future, but it was just noisier. Her body was demanding that she go back to sleep. Since she had no job to get to, and no boyfriend to answer to, she felt no reason to answer the door. Perhaps it was an overzealous sales person. She knew they would give up eventually. She buried her face in her pillow once more and did her best to ignore the pounding.

"Police!" a heavy voice shouted through the door. That one word made her leap right up out of her bed with her heart in her throat. Police? Images of handguns and handcuffs filled her mind.

"Uh! Just a minute!" Wendy called out as she was sure their next step might be to burst through the door. She snatched her robe off her desk chair and pulled it on over the pajama pants and t-shirt she had worn to bed. She was sure she didn't look anywhere near decent, but police didn't tend to care about that. She pulled the door open and stared right into the faces of two police officers. One was tall and thin, the other short and round, and both looked displeased.

"Didn't you hear us knocking?" the shorter officer asked.

"I'm sorry, I was just so tired," Wendy murmured and shook her head, still in a daze as she tried to blink the sleep from her eyes. "What is this about?" she asked nervously.

"I'm Officer Delaney, and this is Officer Polson, we're here to ask you a few questions about your employer, Camilla Blue," he said as he took a step forward, intending to enter the condo.

"Former," Wendy said as she stepped back to allow them both inside. "Camilla let me go two days ago. Is she in some kind of trouble?" Wendy asked, and hoped that there was no glee in her voice. She thought perhaps she had crossed the wrong person and was arrested for assault.

"She's dead," Officer Delaney said flatly as he set his glittering gray eyes on her. "And you were one of the last people to see her alive," he seemed to be gauging her reaction very closely.

"What?" Wendy's eyes widened as the word struck her hard in the gut. "Dead?" she stammered. "But that's impossible!" How could a woman as powerful as Camilla suddenly be dead?

"Is it?" Officer Polson asked and flipped open a notepad. "Where were you last night between the hours of ten and twelve pm?" the officer asked sternly.

"I was here," Wendy said quickly. "Why do you need to know that?" Everything began to fall into place in her mind as Officer Polson made some notes, and Officer Delaney swept his gaze nosily around her condo.

"You live here alone?" he asked skeptically before looking back at her.

"I do now," she answered hesitantly. "My boyfriend moved out recently," she lowered her voice feeling strange for divulging such personal information.

"Oh? Before or after you fought with Camilla Blue, first over her firing you then yesterday over clients?" Polson asked as he studied her closely and even puffed out his chest as if he was attempting to intimidate her.

Wendy's heart sped up until she could barely find a way to breathe. She realized this was more than a friendly visit, this was an investigation, and their prime suspect seemed to be her.

"I didn't fight with her," Wendy corrected defensively.

"There were witnesses," Polson pointed out sternly. "A Marcia Cruz, and a Veronica Timmons," he said before looking back up at her. "Does that seem right to you?"

"Well yes, they were both there at the office when Camilla fired me," Wendy said swiftly as she guessed that Ronnie was short for Veronica. "I mean of course I was upset, I did everything for her, and she just fired me like I was nothing."

"Sounds like you've had an emotional couple of days," Delaney said casually as he strolled into the kitchen. "Do you mind if I get a glass of water?" he asked as his gaze swept over the sink.

"Go ahead," Wendy said grimly. "Yes, it has been hard, but that doesn't mean I had anything to do with Camilla's death!"

"No one said it did, yet," Polson said from

just beside her. "So, when you saw her the day after she fired you and the two of you fought over clients, was that just you being a little upset, too?" he asked and Wendy thought she could sense some sarcasm in his tone.

"They were my clients that I had a meeting with," Wendy pointed out. She attempted to remain calm, but there was panic creeping into her voice. She didn't like to be accused of things. "They were referred by a mutual friend and they would never have used Camilla's company if I wasn't working there. They wanted me to plan their wedding and when I showed up Camilla was telling them that they couldn't work with me anymore. Yes, we had words, and yes, I was upset."

"You even threatened her, isn't that right?" Polson asked with a slight smirk.

"No! I..." Wendy's voice suddenly cut off as she recalled what she had said. "Well, I said some things because I was angry, but I would never hurt her!"

"Sure," Polson nodded and made a note. "So, after losing your job, threatening Camilla, and your boyfriend moving out, I bet you were feeling pretty low," he suggested in an understanding tone.

"I was," Wendy admitted in a whisper, as her mind was growing numb.

"Did you maybe drink a little, use some illegal drugs?" he suggested in a conspiratorial tone. "I mean all of that happening at once was probably a little much to handle."

"What?" Wendy shook her head sharply. "No! I don't drink much and I don't take any kind of drugs."

"Looks like you did some crafting," Delaney said as he picked up the waste basket in the kitchen and showed the contents to Polson.

"Oh, that..." Wendy stammered, her lips growing numb with shock as Delaney pointed out the cut up pictures of Camilla.

"I think we're going to need a warrant," Delaney said calmly. "Ms. Reed, I'd like you to come down to the station to discuss this further."

Wendy stared at him, her stomach lurching. She realized that the evidence was piling up against her. She was going to need a lawyer. She was going to need real pants!

"Can I get dressed first?" she asked hopefully as she looked between the two officers.

"Fine," Polson nodded. "But make it quick, please."

Wendy ducked back into her room and changed quickly. She was sure that once they got down to the station they would be able to straighten all of this out. It had to be a mistake for them to look into her, she hadn't been arrested for anything before let alone murder. Just then it struck her that Camilla was really dead. As angry as she had been at the woman the day before, she couldn't imagine someone hurting her. Who could have done such a thing?

***

The ride to the police station was mortifying. Wendy slumped down low in the back seat of the police car. She was grateful that they hadn't handcuffed her, and they had insisted that she was just going to the precinct for questioning. But she was still terrified. She kept going over and over in her mind the things that she had done in the past few days. The fights with Camilla, the cut up pictures, all added up to look like the wild behavior of someone who might be mentally unstable. She of course knew she wasn't, but would the police accept that?

When they reached the station the two officers led her to an interrogation room. Wendy closed her eyes as they shut the door and left her alone for a few moments. She was trying to get herself under control as she knew that her panic and fear might make her look even more guilty. The clock on the wall was ticking loudly. When she walked into the room she had noticed that it was behind bars, just like she would be, if she said or did the wrong thing.

"I'm innocent," she said softly to herself in an attempt to focus more clearly on that instead of her panic over being escorted by police officers.

"Who are you trying to convince, me or you?" Officer Polson asked as he sat down across from her. With her eyes closed Wendy hadn't even noticed that he came back into the room. She met his eyes, and noticed they were a deep shade of blue, like the sky on a warm summer day.

They could have been kind if he wasn't glowering at her.

"I know that some of this looks bad, but I haven't seen Camilla since yesterday at the resort..."

"Well, how convenient," the officer said as he slid a photograph across the table towards her. "Because that's where we found her. She was shot and then thrown in the water."

Wendy glanced down at the photograph and quickly looked away.

"Please take it away," she whispered as she did not want to look at a Camilla's dead body.

"Hard to look at," he agreed and slid the photograph back into a folder. "But at the time, with all your anger running through you, maybe you just couldn't stop yourself. I get that, people snap, we're only human, and with what you were dealing with, well...I think anyone would snap."

Wendy stared at him with horror in her eyes. "I could never do that," she insisted in a soft, shocked tone. "I could never take someone's life like that," she grimaced as she glanced in the direction of the folder.

"I don't think that you would do it in your right mind," Polson nodded and tapped lightly on the folder. "But maybe your mind got a little lost."

"No," Wendy said firmly. "It didn't. I did not see Camilla again after she left the restaurant. I don't know who did, but it wasn't me."

"Well, that's the thing, we don't know, either," Polson said as he folded his hands on his stomach and sat back in his chair. "Because as far as we can tell you are the only one that threatened her that day. You are the only enemy of Camilla's that we know of."

"I'm not Camilla's enemy," Wendy argued incredulously. Then she sighed as she closed her eyes. "At least I wasn't. Camilla taught me everything I know. I've worked with her for years. Yes, I was angry that she fired me, but no I wouldn't ever do anything to hurt her."

"Except stealing her clients and trying to ruin her business?" Polson suggested with a faint smirk playing at his lips. "Why not go one step further and take her life, too?"

"They were my clients," Wendy offered

though she knew it was fruitless. From the look in the officer's eyes it was clear that he had already made a decision about her. "Are you going to arrest me?" she asked with wide, tear-filled eyes. All of this was just far too overwhelming for her.

He was silent for a long moment as he studied her, before his thin lips drew into an even thinner line.

"Not today," he finally said as he knocked on the table lightly.

"Oh," Wendy blinked back her tears. She wasn't sure if she should be relieved or not. "Can I go?" she asked in a shaky voice.

"There are a few papers to sign," he said calmly and then stood up from his chair. He opened the door to the interrogation room and gestured for her to step out. Wendy was a little nervous to even stand up. From the way he was looking at her, she felt as if he was looking for any reason at all to arrest her. As she walked across the room and out through the door, she could feel his gaze lingering on her. Her breath was short as she expected any moment she might feel the cold grasp of handcuffs around her wrists. She started to walk down the hall that led to the exit, but Polson grabbed her by the elbow before she could. She clenched her teeth and braced herself, expecting that he was going to restrain her.

"Just sit here," he instructed and something about his voice had softened. She glanced over at him as he pointed to a chair for her to wait in. She must have looked terrified, because he looked a little concerned. "It's all right, just some paperwork," he said as he pointed to some papers on the desk. "I'll need you to sign them, okay?"

"Yes," Wendy nodded as she sat down in her chair. Polson walked down the hall, glancing over his shoulder a few times as he did.

Wendy sat alone in the hard, metal chair after scrawling her name on the paperwork. She was trembling. She didn't want to be, but she couldn't help it. As she fumbled with her purse, she noticed someone sitting across from her. Once she laid eyes on him, it was hard to look away. He had a very intriguing manner about him. His legs were casually outstretched before him, encased in old, worn jeans that ran right up to a thick, black belt. On his hip a gun was holstered, though Wendy didn't see any badge. His button-down, blue shirt was tucked into the waistband of his jeans, just snug enough to hint at his abdominal muscles, and accentuate the broadness of his chest. He had his hands folded behind his head as he leaned back in his chair. His chin was covered in the faint scruff of a beard as if he hadn't shaved in a few days. It was not quite as dark as the waves on the top of his head. From his upturned lips a toothpick lazily protruded. Wendy was slightly shocked not to see a cowboy hat on his head as his entire demeanor reminded her of one. It wasn't until he lowered his head to meet her eyes that she realized she was staring at him. His eyes were large and hazel as they hung on her features. She glanced away quickly and tugged at her purse once more.

"Ms. Reed," Officer Polson said as he walked over to her. "We're going to let you go home tonight. But please, stay local, and be available to answer our calls. What is the best number to contact you on?" he asked.

"I," Wendy grimaced as she realized she

didn't even have a phone at the moment. "I don't have a number."

"Don't play games," Polson warned. "I can keep you here if I need to."

"No, please don't," Wendy said quickly, the desperation obvious in her voice. "It's just that Camilla paid for my phone, and she took it back when she fired me, and I haven't gotten another one yet."

"Well, without a way to contact you, we're going to have to keep you," Polson said firmly.

"No please, I'll go and get a phone right now," she insisted and stood up swiftly from the chair, perhaps a little too aggressively.

"I'm sorry, that's not going to work," Polson said as he reached for his handcuffs.

"Calm down, Polson," the man sitting across from her said as he stood up from his chair. He was taller than she had expected. "Here," he handed Polson a business card. "You can reach her here, until she gets her new phone. I'll keep an eye on her for you," he winked lightly at Wendy. Wendy didn't normally enjoy a stranger inserting himself into her business, but she was willing to accept any help she could find at the moment.

"Yes," Wendy nodded quickly. "I'll stay with him."

"You sure about that, Brian?" Polson asked as he took the card from him. Wendy caught sight of the business card as it changed hands.

It showed the man's name in bold print, Brian Alexander, and listed his profession as private investigator. Wendy looked up from the card into Brian's eyes, and he offered her a kind smile.

Wendy felt a small sense of relief.

"Is that all right with you, Ms. Reed?" Brian asked politely.

"Yes," Wendy nodded. "Yes, I'll just run to the nearest shop and pick up a new phone, and I'll call you with the number as soon as I get it," Wendy promised as she looked back at Polson.

"All right," Polson nodded slowly. "But remember, stay local," he reminded her with warning in his tone.

Chapter Four

Wendy's head was spinning as she walked with Brian down the hallway to the exit. Brian was silent until they reached the parking lot.

"You can ride with me," Brian offered as he gestured to a plain black Cadillac that was parked in front of the police station. Wendy didn't have much of a choice since her car was still at her condo, but it was a little strange to get in the car of a complete stranger, especially an armed one.

"Thanks," she said quietly as she opened the passenger side door. When she closed her door behind her, he climbed into the driver's side. She could smell his cologne all over the car. It wasn't strong, just there, as if there was rarely any other smell to disrupt it. Or perhaps he spent a lot of time in his car. He sat behind the tan wheel of the car and didn't move to start it.

"So, why don't you tell me what is going on, Wendy?" he asked as he glanced over at her. She noticed the way he was careful not to look at her directly. She was relieved by that since she felt as if she had just been through hours of interrogation. She knew it hadn't been that long, but it felt that way.

"I'd rather not talk about it," she sighed and laid her head back against the tan material of the car seat. She felt as if her entire body was throbbing with fear. She had never experienced so much panic. Not only in the last two days had she lost two of the things she held very dear in her life, now she might even lose her freedom.

"Just take a deep breath," Brian advised solemnly.

"Huh?" Wendy looked over at him, and met his eyes briefly. They really were quite lovely, shifting from greens to blues, and even looking brownish at times.

"You're scared," he said as he slid the key into the ignition. "It's perfectly normal to be. Just take a deep breath, and let your nerves calm down."

"I'm not scared," she began to argue but her voice faded off completely unconvincing. She took a deep breath as she closed her eyes.

"Did you kill her?" he suddenly asked, the car still idling in the parking lot.

"What?" Wendy snapped, her eyes opening and her breath leaving her lungs at the same time.

He shifted in his seat so he could look directly at her. "Did you kill her?" he pronounced each word carefully.

"Of course not," Wendy replied with growing irritation. "Do I look like a killer to you?"

"One thing I've learned, Wendy, is that a killer rarely looks like a killer," he said coolly and then began backing out of the parking spot. "I only asked, because if you know you're innocent, that should help you to calm down."

"You're right," Wendy agreed with a heavy sigh and gazed out the window. "I shouldn't be scared when I've done nothing wrong."

"I didn't say that," he corrected her as he drove down the road towards a small strip mall that contained a cell phone store. "You have plenty of reason to be scared. From what I've heard, there's a lot of evidence against you. People have been convicted with much less."

"Are you trying to make me feel better, or worse?" she asked as she gritted her teeth and looked in his direction.

"I'm just being honest," he replied and then brushed his fingertips lightly over the crease of his lips just beneath his nose. "You want me to lie to you, I'll tell you that innocent people never go to prison, that circumstantial evidence is thrown out of court, and that cops are never in a rush to close a high profile case."

Wendy's heart sank as she realized he was right. Camilla was a big name in the region, and as long as her murder went unsolved people would be upset and demanding that the police find a suspect. Luckily for them, they had a perfect suspect right in front of them, never mind that she didn't commit the crime. He parked and turned the car off in silence. They sat there for a few moments. Then he looked over at Wendy. Wendy couldn't bear to look at him. He was being kind to her, but she hated him for pointing out the truth.

"How do you know so much about the case?" she asked with suspicion.

"I have connections," he smiled sheepishly.

"I'm going to be arrested, aren't I?" she asked in a whisper without looking in his direction.

"Not if I can help it," he murmured. When she felt his touch on the back of her hand it seemed to inspire calm within her, and even comfort. She glanced up at him.

"Why are you helping me?" she asked hesitantly.

"Because you're not a killer, Wendy," he smiled a little as he pulled his hand away from her. "And you don't deserve to be treated like one. Now, let's get you a phone before Polson sends out a search party."

Wendy drew a deep breath and tried to force down her fear. It was nice to have Brian's assurance but she had only just met him. How could he possibly keep her from being arrested?

***

When Wendy and Brian walked into the shop a woman behind the counter smiled at them. Wendy couldn't smile back. She made her living being cheerful and helpful, but she couldn't muster a good attitude at the moment.

"I'll take this phone," she said quickly to the clerk and handed her one of the phones off the rack. "I just need it up and running as quickly as possible, please."

"Right away," the woman smiled and nodded. As Wendy watched the clerk walk away with what would be her new cell phone, Wendy felt everything come crashing down on her again. It was easy to get lost in the fact that she was questioned by police for murder, but she was also unemployed with bills to pay. She would have enough to buy the phone, but how long would she be able to pay for the service? She didn't exactly have much socked away.

"What am I going to do?" she said under her breath as her chest began to tighten again. "I need to get a lawyer."

"No, what you need is a good private investigator," Brian smiled as he leaned back against the counter. "And lucky for you, you've got one! Now, I don't normally fall for the damsel in distress routine, but it's not hard for me to tell that you wouldn't hurt a fly. So, you're in luck, I'll help you," he shrugged.

Wendy stared at him with disbelief. His casual attitude was one thing, but the fact that he seemed to be waiting for her to jump for joy was quite another.

"I'm no damsel in distress," she said sternly and squared her shoulders. "And what could a private investigator do to help me?"

"I don't know," he stood up from the counter as the clerk returned with Wendy's phone. "Find out who the killer really is?" he suggested.

"Oh," Wendy took the phone from the clerk, who looked at them uncomfortably. She handed the clerk her credit card to pay for the phone and then looked back at Brian. "Do you really think you could do that?"

"No," he replied flatly.

"What? Then why did you offer?" Wendy asked with confusion and accepted her credit card back from the clerk.

"I said I couldn't do it, at least not without your help," he explained as they walked towards the door of the shop.

Wendy stopped outside the shop. The sidewalk was scattered with scraps of garbage and broken glass. It was not the nicest place to be, but as she stood next to Brian she was surprised that she felt safe.

"How can I help?" she asked with a shake of her head. "Everything I've done so far has made things worse."

"Well," he smiled faintly as he squinted through the late morning sun. "You already know who the murderer is."

"No, I don't," Wendy said quickly. "If I did, I wouldn't need your help."

"You do," he insisted and guided her back towards the car. "You just don't realize it. So you and I are going to get to the bottom of this together."

"I don't know," Wendy frowned. "Can I get into trouble by doing this?"

"No," he said firmly and opened the car door for her. "I'm going to make sure you stay out of handcuffs, Wendy, understand?"

Wendy wanted to believe him. The way the corners of his eyes crinkled as he stared so convincingly at her, and the firm grasp he had on the door he held open, made her think that he was being honest. But just because he said he would do his best to help her, didn't mean she wouldn't be locked away for a long time.

"Thank you," she finally managed to say. "For helping me."

"Don't thank me just yet," he chuckled a little and closed the door after she had slid inside. As they drove back to Wendy's condo she called Polson to give him her new contact number. She also called Brenda and John to make sure they had her number. She had called so many times in the past that she knew their number off by heart. It went to voicemail.

"Brenda, this is Wendy I just want you to know I have a new number in case you need to reach me," she hung up the phone and Brian glanced over at her but didn't say a word. As they neared her condo, Wendy was reminded of how empty it would be. It was strange how Aaron walking away had seemed like such a devastating moment only a day ago, but now all she could think of was her life unfolding inside a jail cell.

"Do you want me to walk you in?" he offered,

jolting her from her thoughts. She hadn't even realized they were parked.

"No, it's fine," she replied shyly and released her seat belt.

"You've been through a lot today," he said quietly. "I'll find out what I can from the police, and do some digging. But first thing tomorrow you and I need to start digging in your mind. You were Camilla's assistant, you knew everyone she did. You're going to be the one who knows who killed her."

"You keep saying that," Wendy smiled wryly. "I just hope it's true."

As she left the car she shuddered a little. A part of her hoped it wasn't true. She didn't want to think that she could have ever laid eyes on anyone that would kill Camilla.

As she walked up to the condo she was a little surprised to find someone standing in front of her door. She recognized the woman by her perfect hair as she turned to face Wendy.

"Wendy, right?" Veronica asked as she tilted her head slightly to the side.

Wendy immediately felt the air getting

sucked right out of her lungs. This was Veronica, a woman that Camilla had considered her niece, a woman who had taken over Wendy's job and who had told the police about the argument between Camilla and Wendy two days before. What was she doing outside her house? Whatever it was Wendy didn't think it could be anything good.

"Yes," Wendy choked out and took a slight step back. "I'm sorry about Camilla," she said quickly and looked nervously around to see if anyone else was nearby. She didn't want another argument to unfold that would make her look even worse in the eyes of the law.

"That's why I'm here," Veronica said with a slow sigh. "Would you mind getting a drink with me?"

"Uh, what?" Wendy shifted from one foot to the other and adjusted her purse on her shoulder. She didn't think it would be right to share a drink with Veronica considering that Wendy had just been questioned as a suspect in Camilla's murder, but Veronica didn't seem to think anything of it.

"Please, I just moved into town, and I don't

know anyone else. I really need to talk to someone," Veronica insisted. "Just one glass of wine and then I'll be out of your hair, I promise," she looked pleadingly at Wendy.

"All right," Wendy heard herself answer, though she couldn't figure out why she agreed. The last thing she needed was wine to loosen her emotions even more. But maybe the idea of going back into her empty condo was enough motivation, or the fact that Veronica seemed as if she could really use a friend.

"Let's go," Wendy nodded. "I'll meet you at Bally's. Do you know where it is?"

"Yes, that's fine," Veronica nodded and walked off to her car. As Wendy walked over to her own vehicle her mind was swimming yet again. Maybe it was a mistake to go for a drink with Veronica, but anything more she could learn about Camilla would probably be helpful, and Veronica probably knew a lot more than Wendy ever did.

The bar was quiet as it was early afternoon. They found a table near the back door, and the two women looked awkwardly at each other.

"Thanks for joining me," Veronica said with a frown.

"I think you should know that I had nothing to do with Camilla's death," Wendy said swiftly.

"What?" Veronica narrowed her eyes. "Of course you didn't. You don't exactly strike me as a killer."

Wendy lifted her eyebrows, and wondered what she was lacking that made her look so innocent. Then she wondered why she was offended that no one would think of her as a killer.

"Well, I just wanted to say something, because I was at the police station today discussing the case," Wendy explained as the waitress walked over to take their drink orders.

"Two white wines," Veronica ordered for them. Wendy didn't complain, she didn't drink often enough to have a preferred drink. As the waitress walked away Veronica looked back at her. "You know I didn't even have many people to call. The cops contacted me first. It's just so odd," she shook her head. "One day she's giving me a job, the next she's dead."

"It's a terrible tragedy," Wendy said softly as she accepted the white wine from the waitress. Veronica accepted hers as well and then fixed Wendy with a steady stare.

"Let's be honest about this, shall we?" Veronica asked as she sipped her white wine. "Camilla wasn't exactly a saint to be grieved over."

"Excuse me?" Wendy asked with a growing frown. She was sure that she couldn't have heard Veronica correctly.

"She was a cruel, selfish, and heartless woman," Veronica declared and then polished off the last of her white wine.

"How can you say that when she gave you a job?" Wendy asked with a touch of irritation. It was her job she had been given after all.

"Do you know why she gave me that job?" Veronica asked as she looked across the table at Wendy.

"Because you're like a niece to her," Wendy replied hesitantly, she didn't want to offend Veronica by implying she was not qualified for the job, but the truth was, she wasn't.

"Because she slept with my father, and broke up my parents' marriage," Veronica corrected her sharply. "She seduced him, because she can't stand my mother having anything she can't have. That's the reason she gave me the job, because she felt guilty, and because she wanted me to move away from my mother, because Camilla wanted me to be closer to her," she rolled her eyes.

"Wow," Wendy murmured and lowered her gaze. She knew that Camilla could be cold, but she had no idea that she would stoop to such levels. "I didn't know that."

"Well, not too many people do," Veronica sighed and ordered another glass of wine. "My mother always covered it up. She would go on and on about what a great person Camilla was and how generous she had been to our family. But I could tell that she didn't believe it. She was just saying it so the checks would keep rolling in. Camilla would send money to flaunt her wealth, and to appease my mother. Well, my mother was her only friend," Veronica shrugged and met Wendy's eyes. "So, Camilla didn't get her way for once," Veronica shook her head and chuckled as another glass of wine was placed in front of her. "Seems a little bit like justice and a little less like tragedy, doesn't it?" she asked with a light wink as she looked up at Wendy.

Wendy didn't know what to say. As much as she loathed Camilla for the way she had treated her, she also couldn't think of anyone being murdered as justice.

"I think maybe you've had too much," Wendy said as she reached for the glass of wine to take it from Veronica.

"Hey, I can drink as much as I want," Veronica shot back and snatched the glass before Wendy could take it away. "I'm not the murder suspect here."

Wendy's jaw clenched in reaction to those words. She stood up from the table.

"I had nothing to do with Camilla's death, Veronica," she said sternly.

"That's too bad, because if you had," Veronica smirked as she took another gulp from the glass. "I would have bought you another drink."

Wendy frowned as she walked away from the

table. Veronica was harboring so much animosity towards Camilla. Was it possible that she had taken the opportunity to finally punish her for her sins?

Wendy glanced back over her shoulder uneasily and saw that Veronica had ordered yet another glass of wine. Was it possible that Veronica carried such a bitterness inside of her that it had driven her to kill Camilla?

Chapter Five

As Wendy waited for Brian to arrive she poured herself a glass of water. She added a few ice cubes which clinked against the side of her glass, disrupting the silence in the apartment. It brought up a reminder of Aaron's absence. She hadn't really had time to process it. She sighed as she carried the glass of water into the living room. She had already laid out a notebook, some pens, and her laptop on the coffee table. She was determined to make some progress on figuring out who had committed the murder.

Time was ticking, and Wendy knew that she was still the main focus of the investigation. She checked her phone and saw that it had been an hour since she had texted Brian. She frowned and dialed his number. It rang several times. Then she heard it ringing just outside her door. She walked over to it and opened it to find Brian standing there with the phone in his one hand and a bag of Chinese food in the other.

"Honey chicken?" he offered with that slight smile that reminded Wendy of a cat that always landed on its feet.

"I'm about to go to prison for murder," Wendy said with impatience. "I really don't care about Chinese food."

"You should," he said as he walked into the condo. "They don't serve honey chicken in prison."

Wendy stared at him incredulously as he sidled over to the living room and set the bag down on the coffee table. When he glanced up to find her still standing there, staring at him, he cracked a half-smile.

"I'm joking. I stopped in to talk to the people at the restaurant because Camilla's credit card information showed it was the last purchase she made. Since I was there, I thought I'd pick us up some dinner," he paused a moment as Wendy reluctantly stepped closer. "Don't think for a second that I'm not taking this seriously," he said, his entire demeanor shifting from playful and charming to one of complete determination.

"Did you find out anything of interest at the restaurant?" Wendy asked and walked into the kitchen to get them some drinks.

"I found out that Camilla bought a dinner for

two at seven pm, so about three hours before her death, she was either binge eating or sharing a meal with someone," he said as he sat down on the couch and accepted the glass of water she brought him.

"Camilla never binged on anything," Wendy said with a slight roll of her eyes. "She counted her calories right down to the breath mint."

"Wow," he shook his head and furrowed a brow. "That's something I'll never understand."

"Well, be glad you don't have to," Wendy replied with a light smile.

"Wait, what was that?" he asked and stared at her intently.

"What was what?" she asked in return, a little confused.

"Was that a smile I just saw, or did you just have an itch?" he raised his eyebrows and smiled broadly, turning his charm right back on.

"I'm sorry, I wasn't aware that someone being accused of murder should be cheerful," Wendy pointed out but she couldn't help smiling again, and this time wider.

"I know you're under a lot of stress," he replied soothingly and handed her an egg roll. "But whether you're smiling or frowning won't change anything. We're going to get this figured out, you just have to trust me."

"But I barely know you," Wendy reminded him and then bit into the egg roll.

"That can change," he said quietly and when he looked up at her again his expression had shifted into a more sincere one. "I want to help you, Wendy. But to do that, you're going to have to relax, and let me find out what you've got hidden in that mind of yours."

"I know you think I know who the killer is, but I just don't see how that's possible," Wendy frowned and stared down at the glossy chicken in the container before her. She really did love honey chicken.

"Eat first," he suggested. "It's easier to pick a well-fed brain."

Wendy smiled a little at his comment. His boisterous personality was beginning to rub off on her. She found herself really smiling again for the first time in what seemed like a lifetime, but was only a few days. As she ate her honey chicken, she kept glancing over at him. The slope of his jaw and the curve of his chin made his profile very handsome.

"So, what made you become a private investigator?" Wendy abruptly asked. She felt as if he knew so much about her, while she knew nothing about him. Sitting beside him in her living room, sharing Chinese food, it just didn't seem right to have no idea of who he was.

"Honestly, I wanted to be a cop," he explained with a shy shrug before picking up his egg roll and taking a bite.

"And?" Wendy asked, as it appeared he had no intention of continuing to speak.

"Well, there was one problem," he offered her a rakish grin, his eyes mischievous as he looked at her.

"What was that?" Wendy asked intrigued by what might have been his stumbling block.

"Cops have to play by the rules," he explained with a short laugh. "The first time I was expected to drop and give twenty, I walked right out of the academy," he lowered his voice a little. "I don't deal well with authority."

"Oh," Wendy's eyes widened as he took another bite of his egg roll. As laid back and sarcastic as he seemed to be, she was beginning to sense that he might be a bit of a loose cannon. If that was the case she wasn't sure if she should be relying on him to solve the murder. "But don't you think a little order, some uniform rules, are important?" she asked.

"Not when it comes to guilt and innocence," he said firmly and laid down his chopsticks. He turned on the couch so he could face her. "I've seen quite a few people go free on a technicality, or go to jail on invalid evidence. I knew as a police officer there wasn't much I could do about that, but as a private investigator I could do a lot more."

"That makes sense," Wendy nodded cautiously. "I guess you've seen quite a lot so far," she added as she studied him. He appeared to be in his early thirties.

"I have," he agreed. "But you're the first person I volunteered to help. Usually my clients come looking for me."

"But I can't afford to pay you at the moment," Wendy said apologetically. "I will when I can, though."

"Don't worry about it," he replied dismissively

"I just can't believe all of this is happening," Wendy said sadly as she sat back on the couch.

"As much as I'd like to tell you that you can ignore all of this and it will go away, that's not going to happen..." his words were interrupted by Wendy's new cell phone ringing.

Wendy glanced at her phone to find that it was Brenda calling her. She picked it up quickly.

"Hi, Wendy?" Brenda asked anxiously. "I wasn't sure if this was your new number or not."

"It is," Wendy replied warmly. "How are you?"

"Well, honestly, I'm falling apart," Brenda confessed and Wendy could hear the tears in her voice. "I know this is incredibly selfish of me after what happened to Camilla, but you are the only one who knows just how I want everything at the wedding, and the wedding is on Sunday, and I..."

"Brenda, take a deep breath," Wendy coaxed her. Brian shifted on the couch and glanced over at her with concern.

Wendy could hear Brenda taking a deep breath and then exhaling into the phone.

"Wendy, will you please help me?" Brenda begged.

"Of course, I will," Wendy assured her. "Let's meet first thing in the morning, okay?"

"Oh, really? Oh, thank you so much, Wendy!" Brenda gushed into the phone. "You have no idea how relieved I am. Are you sure?"

"Yes, you're going to have the wedding of your dreams, Brenda, I promise you," as soon as the words left Wendy's lips she regretted speaking them. How could she promise Brenda the wedding of her dreams when she might be in jail by Sunday?

"Everything okay?" Brian asked as he met her eyes.

"I think so," Wendy sighed. "I just have to find a way to make this wedding work."

"Well, before you can do that, we need to

figure out who killed Camilla," he reminded her.

"The only person that comes to mind is Veronica," she nodded her head thoughtfully. She had already explained to him what she had said over the drink they had together. "But why would she be so open about her hatred if she killed her?"

"I'll still look into it," he nodded. "But we need to give the police as many suspects as possible."

"But how?" Wendy shook her head. "I've been thinking about it, but I can't figure out who it could be."

"You're so tense with all of this, you're probably blocking out the obvious," Brian suggested. "Just lean back on the couch and get comfortable."

Wendy didn't want to tell him that he was adding to her tension by sliding closer to her on the couch.

"Now just try to relax," he instructed as Wendy sat back against the couch. "Listen to the sound of my voice," he added, and his voice became smooth and soothing. "There's a lot going on in your mind," he continued. "We need to get past all of that, to what happened in the days before Camilla's death."

"Okay," Wendy murmured. With her eyes closed, her mind was spinning. It was filled with the fear of handcuffs, thoughts of Brenda's wedding, moments of Camilla's laughter, the glass of white wine in Veronica's hand, and Marcia's expression when Camilla fired her. All of it was a jumble, and she didn't see how she would ever get through it. Then she felt Brian's hand come to rest gently on the back of hers. She tensed for a moment at the physical connection. His hand was a lot softer than she had expected it to be, and he didn't rest the full weight of it against her, just a soft anchoring touch.

"Take a slow breath," he instructed. "And relax," he continued as she drew in her breath. "I want you to think about last week. Was there anything happening last week that had you concerned? Any arguments? Any confrontations with Camilla?"

"Just the usual," Wendy replied in a softened voice.

"What usual?" Brian pressed and leaned a

little closer.

"Anything that went wrong in Camilla's life, she came to me to solve," Wendy explained. "So, last week she lost one of her favorite shoes, needed her sandwich returned because it had too many seeds on the crust, wanted her hairstylist fired because of a mishap with a bobby pin, and of course there were the clients that were specifically requesting me over her," she explained. "It was nothing out of the ordinary. I think I'd remember if something truly threatening occurred."

Brian sighed and rubbed a hand across his eyes before glancing at his watch.

"Here's the situation. We only have so much time before the police are going to take a shot at arresting you. Even if we can think of other suspects that we can throw out as a possibility, you'd have a better chance of avoiding handcuffs."

Wendy stared down at her hands which had begun to tremble again. "I'm trying," she murmured. "I really am."

Brian frowned and laid one hand over one of

hers. "I know you are. I'm not trying to scare you, I just want you to be prepared."

"Thanks," she sighed. Before she could speak again her cell phone rang again. She saw that it was Brenda.

"Wendy, we need to stay focused on this..." Brian began to say, but Wendy had already answered the phone.

"What's happening, Brenda?" she asked.

"I just called to confirm the roses for tomorrow, and the florist said they didn't get their delivery, and if we don't have the roses by tomorrow then nothing will be decorated, and if nothing is decorated it's not really a wedding, is it? Not a real wedding..." she continued to gush, her anxiety clear in her voice.

"Brenda, everything's going to be fine," Wendy promised her. "I'll take care of the flowers, you get a glass of wine and snuggle up with John, okay?"

"Are you sure?" Brenda asked with a sniffle in her voice. "I mean there's still so much to do!"

"It's all under control," Wendy assured her. "Nothing is going to stop you from having the wedding of your dreams."

"Oh, thank you so much, Wendy, thank you," Brenda sighed into the phone before hanging up.

Wendy hung up her cell phone and quickly began a web search to find local florists that could provide the roses that Brenda was looking for. She would be able to get a refund from the original florist which would offset the cost of the new roses.

"Wendy," Brian said impatiently as she sorted through the results.

"Just a minute," she said and held up one finger before scrolling. She was familiar with most of the florists but Camilla had a contract with many of them. She had to find one that wasn't involved with Camilla before her death so there wouldn't be any issues getting the roses.

"Wendy," Brian said again more impatiently, his voice rising slightly. "Do you know how important it is that we find out what really happened to Camilla? There might already be an arrest warrant out for you!"

"I know, I know," Wendy said with a slight nod and then smiled as she found the florist she was looking for. She touched the button to dial the number immediately and then glanced over at Brian.

"It's okay, just let me make this one call," she said with a small smile.

"Unbelievable," Brian shook his head. "Isn't your freedom more important than a wedding?" he asked.

"No," she replied simply.

"How can you say that?" he gasped and stared at her with wide eyes.

"Hold on," she shushed him and began ordering the roses. "I need them by tomorrow morning. Yes, I understand, I'll cover the fee. Just make sure they are pink, okay? Great, thank you," she said swiftly before hanging up the phone.

"Wendy," Brian reached for her phone. "You need to turn that over until we get this situation straightened out. You could be in handcuffs at any time."

"But I'm not," she pointed out as she swiftly tucked the phone back into her purse and out of his reach. "And until I am I'm going to make sure that Brenda has the wedding of her dreams."

"That just doesn't make any sense," he complained with a slight shake of his head. "If you really wanted to save yourself from this mess you wouldn't be distracting yourself with this wedding."

"It's not a distraction," Wendy said firmly.

"How can you say that? You're in a dire situation, Wendy, and you're stopping to take calls and call florists," his tone was more urgent than angry, but Wendy noticed the ripple of his jaw. "I'm fighting hard to get you out of this, Wendy, I expect you to do the same," he pointed out gruffly.

"I am doing the same," Wendy assured him. "But Brenda only gets one day, you know?" she smiled faintly. "It's one day that she and her husband will look back on for the rest of their lives."

Brian stared at her thoughtfully. "I guess I never looked at it that way."

"That's okay, not everyone does," Wendy said with a shrug. "Most people see my job as just that, a job. I see it as an opportunity to create that perfect moment for a couple."

"Isn't all that fluff and sparkle just an illusion though?" Brian asked as he looked into her eyes. "Aren't you setting them up for a let down after all the fanfare dies down?"

"I don't think so," Wendy said with a shake of her head. "I can't create what isn't there. No amount of doves, lace, or violins will force love into a wedding. The love has to be there to begin with, everything else is just an expression of it."

Brian seemed to be mildly enchanted by her words, though he still had a skeptical gleam in his eyes. Noting this, she continued with her explanation.

"They will tell their kids about this day. The way they felt on the day might even impact the way they feel during their marriage, do you understand that?" she looked up at him curiously and searched his eyes. "Doesn't that seem important to you?"

"I guess, I never really thought about it too much," he admitted with a slight smile. "The way you describe it makes it sound so special. I've always thought of marriage as one of those things you have to do," he shrugged a little.

"Wow," Wendy said as she looked at him. It always surprised her how cynical some people are about the idea of marriage. "Have you done it?" Wendy asked as he leaned forward on the couch to box up his Chinese food.

"Marriage?" he asked with slightly widened eyes. "No, I can't say I have. I've done my best to avoid it."

"Really?" Wendy asked and was surprised when she felt a slight sense of disappointment. Was she connecting with Brian a little too much? Was she expecting something more from him?

"Well, it's not for everyone," he pointed out and shook his head. "I guess I've never thought of myself as husband material."

"I don't think there's any right husband," Wendy replied in a soft whimsical tone. "I should say, any right way to be a husband. The man you fall in love with, is the right man for you, and life kind of forms around it."

"Well, tell that to the divorce statistics," he chuckled a little as he stood up from the couch.

"It's true, it's rare for a couple to stay

together these days," she said quietly and glanced wistfully over her apartment.

"Oh, I'm sorry," he mumbled and flushed as he realized his mistake. "That was a little insensitive, considering."

"No, it's fine," Wendy shrugged and smiled to reassure him. "The truth is I do believe that if you wait for the right person, you get the magic," she smiled a little at that. "The hard part is waiting, and knowing when to face the fact that the person you're with isn't the right one for you."

"I guess I've never felt that way about anyone I've been with," Brian admitted with a frown. "I suppose my romantic nature is stunted," he laughed at that.

"Sounds like it," Wendy grinned, and felt a quick rush at being amused. Despite the tension of the situation, she was glad that Brian was able to keep things light. "Then of course there are the ones who con you," she rolled her eyes at that.

"Like Aaron?" Brian asked without taking his eyes off her. "Did he con you?" There was a spark of curiosity in his eyes.

"No, not like Aaron," Wendy shook her head and brushed a few of her curls back behind her ear. "Aaron never really led me on. I just saw what I wanted to see in him instead of recognizing what was there," she sighed. "There was this man, a client. A serial bachelor, a real con artist," she pursed her lips with disgust.

"What do you mean a serial bachelor?" Brian asked.

"He's been married more than three times already, Camilla and I planned his two previous weddings. He hooks up with women who are well off, gets them to marry him, then divorces them within months so he can get some of their fortune, and turns around and does it again."

"Sounds like a terrible person," Brian remarked.

"He is," Wendy nodded. "When I saw him show up for the third time, I knew exactly what he was up to. So, I looked into it a little more and it seemed pretty obvious that he was just marrying his new fiancée for her money. There were other marriages before he used our services as well as some information on investments he arranged that fell through. Investors lost all their money and accused him of deceiving them but from what I could tell they couldn't prove any wrong doing and it hasn't been taken any further. "

"You must be quite the detective," Brian arched an eyebrow as if he was impressed. "So, what did you do with what you found?"

"I gave it to Camilla," Wendy replied thoughtfully. "She said she would handle it, come to think of it, I don't know if she ever actually did."

"Wait," Brian looked at her "Are you saying that you found evidence against this guy, and Camilla was going to confront him with it?"

"Well, I'm not sure what she was going to do with it. Maybe just tell the bride-to-be to warn her," Wendy nodded as she slowly began to put the pieces together. "Are you thinking that he might somehow be involved?"

"If he was trying to make himself another million and Camilla threatened to steal that chance, I think it makes him a pretty good suspect," Brian said with growing confidence.

"I don't know," Wendy said with a frown.

"He's not a good guy, but a murderer? I guess it's hard for me to believe that anyone would do something so extreme."

"They do," Brian said as he picked up his leftover Chinese. "Let's pick this up in the morning, first thing? Okay?"

"Sure," Wendy nodded as she stood up as well.

"Can you text me the name of that serial bachelor?" Brian requested as she walked him to the door. "I want to do a little digging on him."

"Sure, no problem," Wendy nodded quickly. "And there's Veronica as well. She sure is carrying a lot of anger and resentment for Camilla."

"Yep," Brian nodded. "I am going to do some digging on her, too," he hesitated in the doorway and turned back to look at her. "Try and get some rest, okay?"

"I will," Wendy promised and then smiled at him as he turned to leave. When she closed the door she rested her forehead against it. She could still feel him standing just outside. Or maybe, like everything she was feeling growing between herself and Brian it was only her imagination. As she turned to put her food away, she felt a new wave of tension flood through her. She didn't have time to be thinking about what Brian might be feeling, he certainly wasn't going to be interested in a felon.

It was impossible for her to even think about sleeping so she settled down on the couch with her computer and began going over the details of Brenda's wedding. She didn't want anything too extravagant but the things she did want had sentimental meaning to her. Wendy was determined to make the wedding a special occasion, even if it meant she had to do it from behind bars.

Chapter Six

Early the next morning Wendy met up with Brenda and John at the resort where they planned to be married. It was the day before the wedding, and Wendy knew that Brenda was on edge.

"Oh, Wendy, the flowers were delivered, thank you so much," Brenda said as she hugged her.

"No problem," Wendy managed a genuine smile despite the fact that she knew at any second Officer Polson could burst through the door to arrest her. "Is everything else going smoothly?"

"Yes, so far so good," Brenda nodded.

"I've double checked with the caterer and also confirmed the time for the delivery of the cake," Wendy said swiftly. "I don't think there's anything to worry about. So now, the two of you can enjoy your rehearsal dinner tonight. But don't stay up too late!"

"We won't," John chuckled. "Not with a

wedding at noon to prepare for."

"It's going to be so perfect," Brenda sighed happily. "I don't know how you do it, Wendy, but thank you for all of your help."

"I don't do it," Wendy said with an affectionate smile. "The two of you are creating this day, don't forget that. You two just relax and enjoy each other's company today, okay? Go for a stroll on the beach, get a little time alone together."

"That sounds wonderful," John murmured and kissed Brenda lovingly on the cheek.

"We'll do that," Brenda nodded and hugged John warmly.

As Wendy was turning away from the couple she nearly walked right into Brian. When she looked up at him, he had a slight scowl.

"I thought we were meeting first thing?" he reminded her. "I went by your condo, but you weren't there."

"How did you find me?" Wendy asked with surprise and nervousness.

"I am an investigator," he reminded her and

guided her towards the door of the resort. "I heard you say everything was set up for the wedding, so now can we focus on keeping you out of jail?"

"Yes, I'd like that very much," Wendy grinned, but her grin faded with Brian's serious expression.

"I just heard from Polson. I bought you some time, Wendy, but the time is going to run out eventually," his hazel eyes were hard as they studied her. "It might be hard to face this, but this is not a game, and it can't be swept under the rug."

"Okay," Wendy breathed and closed her eyes briefly. "So, what can we do?"

"Well, I looked a little deeper into Veronica, and she has an alibi for the time of Camilla's death. She was in the hotel bar until closing," he frowned.

"Oh," Wendy winced. "I guess that doesn't look too good for me."

"We need another person we can point to as a possible killer," Brian explained through gritted teeth. "The more possible suspects the better."

"I can only think of Giuseppe," Wendy shook her head as they walked through the parking lot of the resort.

"Yes, I did some digging on him and he certainly has a colorful past. We do need to speak to him and maybe some of your other clients as well," Brian suggested as he ran his hand across his face and sighed. "Maybe if we interview them we can find something that we're missing."

"We could except that I don't have any of my old contact information," Wendy explained with a frown. "It was all on my cell phone, which was given to Veronica," she stepped out onto the sand that stretched out towards the water.

"And she might not exactly be willing to cooperate with us," Brian nodded a little as he dug one foot a little deeper into the sand. "Wait, did you say that everything was on the cell phone?" he asked.

"Yes," Wendy nodded. "I just thought it was easier to keep it all on the phone because the phone was always on me."

"Perfect!" he snapped his fingers. "Most cell

phone companies have begun storing data on the internet for their customers to access in case their phone has a problem. I think we can get you in there," he grabbed her by the wrist and pulled her back towards the parking lot. "We need to get back to your condo, I'll meet you there."

Wendy was relieved that she might be able to access the information, but she also couldn't ignore the very real sensation of sparks carrying from where Brian's hand was touching her skin, straight up to the top of her head in a sudden wave.

She tried to focus on driving as she followed behind his car, but the memory of his sudden touch was hard to ignore. When she parked he was already standing beside the door of her condo. She unlocked it and opened the door to let him step inside.

As she crossed the threshold behind him, she caught sight of his shadow on her wall. Something about it made her stomach flip.

"Where's your computer?" he asked with urgency in his voice.

"Here," Wendy said quickly and walked over to her computer to set it up for him. As she was opening it up she could feel his presence beside her. She was more than a little surprised by the way he had such an impact on her. She tried to remind herself that it was just because the situation was so emotionally charged. He was no white knight, and as she had already told him once, she was no damsel in distress.

"Let's see," he said as he sat down on the couch beside her and began typing away at the laptop on the coffee table. "Now, we just need an account number..."

"I've got that," Wendy said as she leaned over to type in the numbers. Her hand accidentally brushed against his, and she froze for a moment.

"What's wrong? Did you forget it?" he asked as he turned to look at her. She glanced over at him and their faces were only inches apart. She was caught in his hazel eyes, lost for a moment between the shades of blues and greens.

"No, I remember," she murmured as a strawberry blonde curl fell between them, breaking the trance. "Sorry," she cleared her throat and began typing in the numbers. He sat perfectly still beside her, and she didn't dare to look in his direction to see if he had felt the connection that she did. She reminded herself that she had thought the same thing about Aaron, or at least she thought she did, and that had not turned out very well.

"Here," she announced when the account information logged in correctly. "Now, how do I..." she paused, her voice caught in her throat.

"What is it?" he asked as he leaned a little closer so that he could see the screen as well.

"This isn't my information, it's Camilla's," she said in a whisper. "And look at this," she pointed to the listing of text messages that had popped up. They were mostly from Camilla's number to one other number. Most of the messages were threatening.

"I know what you're up to, and I'm not letting you get away with it again," Brian read out loud.

"If you won't tell her I will," Wendy read next. The texts continued on like that for some time.

"Do you think these are to Giuseppe?" Brian asked anxiously. He pulled out his cell phone and dialed the number that was listed. He listened for a moment, and then nodded his head before he hung up the phone. "It is his number."

"Look, he only responded to her once," Wendy pointed out. "It says, meet me after closing, in 3-A. We can discuss a payment."

"A payment?" Brian asked with surprise. "Do you think he was planning to bribe her?"

"Look at the time," Wendy hissed and pointed to the time stamp beside the text. "It was almost eight-thirty."

"Which makes Giuseppe the last person to have contact with Camilla before her death," Brian said with surprise growing in his voice.

"She was going to keep his secret and let him marry that women, possibly ruin her life," Wendy said with a gasp. "I want to say she wouldn't have let it happen for any amount of money, but," she hesitated for a moment.

"But she wouldn't have minded lining her purse," Brian supplied for her. "Is there anything about a time?"

"No, just after closing, in 3-A," Wendy sighed and sat back against the couch.

"3-A," Brian repeated. "Where do you think that is?"

"I'm not sure," Wendy shook her head. "It could be anywhere. But 3-A," she repeated it again and closed her eyes as there was something familiar about it.

"It has to be a place that closes, so it wouldn't be a storage locker, or anything out in the open," Brian mused as he rubbed his chin slowly. "We're so close now, we can't lose track. The fact that he didn't tell Camilla where it was, means that he already knew that she knew where it was."

"Yes," Wendy nodded as she stared at the screen. Then suddenly she took a sharp breath. "Wait, 3-A, I know where that is!"

"Where is it?" Brian asked as Wendy jumped up from the couch.

"It's at the Sun Resort where Brenda and John are getting married..." her voice trailed off and then she nodded. "It's where Giuseppe's wedding was planned. Camilla and I were there the day she died. There's a conference room we use as a planning space, it's 3-A."

"That's it," Brian said with excitement as he stood up from the couch as well. "That's it, Wendy, you figured it out!" he said and encircled her shoulders with his arms as he pulled her into a celebratory hug. Wendy stopped breathing for a few seconds. She was enveloped in the warmest place she had ever experienced. It had very little to do with body heat, and everything to do with the way she felt inside when he was hugging her. Her heart fluttered, and she took a deep breath. She pulled away from Brian and turned away.

"I'm sorry," he said abruptly. "Did I make you feel uncomfortable?" he was frowning when she looked back at him. "I got a little carried away. It's just that with this information we might find some proof that Giuseppe is the one who killed Camilla. I mean, we could have an entire crime scene that hasn't been investigated."

Wendy stared at him, wondering if that was all that had inspired the hug. She felt as if she was letting her emotions get away from her, yet again.

"No, it's okay," she managed a smile. "It just

surprised me, and I want to check out this lead," she added.

He studied her for a long moment as if he didn't quite believe her, but after a moment he seemed to refocus on the case.

"I think we should see if we can track him down, get his side before he senses that we're onto him," Brian suggested. "Does that sound good to you?"

"Tracking him down might be hard," Wendy said with a cluck of her tongue as she suddenly remembered something. "I think he was due to be married yesterday. He decided to use another venue that has their own dedicated wedding planner, and if the wedding went ahead then he is likely on his honeymoon, which knowing his wife's available funds is probably out of the country."

"Hmm," Brian frowned. "Well, let's see what we can find out, either way."

"Here," she sat back down and jotted down Giuseppe's name, his wife's name, and the location of their wedding. "Why don't you see if your connections can get anything about

Giuseppe's whereabouts from this," she said and slid the paper towards him. "I want to meet up with Veronica again."

"Are you sure?" he asked as he picked up the piece of paper. "She may still be involved in all of this. Do you think it's wise to see her alone?"

"I think I'm running out of time," Wendy said in a serious tone as she met his eyes. "If Giuseppe is out of the country, the focus of the police is still going to be on me. I don't want to go to jail, Brian, I'm just not cut out for it."

"I don't think anyone is," he reminded her with a soft smile. "Don't worry, I'll track him down, and we'll get to the bottom of this. Just make sure you call me if you get into any situation you're not sure of, understand?"

"Yes," Wendy nodded as they walked towards the door of her condo. "I'm not interested in dying either."

"I hope not," he said calmly as he stepped outside the door and then held it open for her. "You do have a wedding to plan after all."

Wendy smiled at that. She walked towards her car, and did her best not to look back over her shoulder. But after the way he had embraced her, all she could think of was wanting him to do it again. It wasn't even an attraction, so much as it was a fascination. That was the real reason she was splitting apart from him to investigate things. She was worried if she stayed beside him much longer she would demand another hug, and that could be awkward, considering his hug probably meant nothing more than a reaction of celebration.

After Wendy started her car she texted Veronica to ask her to meet her at Camilla's office. She wanted to look through Camilla's notes and desk to see if she had left any more information about Giuseppe. More than that she wanted to see if Veronica knew anything about Giuseppe being a conman, because if she did, she might be in danger.

Chapter Seven

When Wendy arrived at the office she still hadn't received a text back from Veronica. She wasn't even sure if Veronica was still in town or if she had gone back home to be with her mother. However, when she walked up to the door of the office she found it slightly ajar. Instantly, Wendy's nerves were set on edge. From the scratching on the metal frame it looked as if the door might have been forced open. She narrowed her eyes and peered through the small opening. She didn't see anything but the long hallway that led back to Camilla's inner office. She listened closely in an attempt to detect whether there was anyone still inside. At first there was only silence. Then she heard something that sounded like knocking. It was followed by a muffled cry. Wendy's heart began to race as she wondered what was happening. Her adrenaline flooded her to the point where it was difficult for her to breathe.

"Hello?" she called out hesitantly. She heard the banging and the muffled cry again. With her stomach in knots Wendy crept into the office.

She had never considered herself brave, but then, she had never had a reason to be before. As she walked past the entrance she grabbed an umbrella from the stand beside the door. She gripped it tightly in her hand as she moved quietly down the hallway. When she reached Camilla's office the first thing she noticed was everything in disarray all over the floor. Her desk was tipped over, as were the chairs. Her filing cabinets had been completely emptied and one was leaning against the other, threatening to make them both fall over. There were pens with the company's name printed on them scattered in all directions. Wendy froze in the doorway and held the umbrella above her head.

"Who's in here?" she demanded.

The banging came again, this time Wendy could tell that it was coming from behind the overturned desk. She inched her way forward until she reached the desk. Then she peered over it, uncertain of what she might find. Was it a trap?

"Marcia!" Wendy gasped when she saw the woman tied and gagged behind the desk. She rushed over to her and tugged at the tape over her mouth until it came free. Marcia let out a loud scream at the pain of having the tape pulled off her skin, and then began crying. From the red and puffy state of her eyes, Wendy could guess that she had been crying for quite some time.

"Marcia, are you okay?" Wendy asked urgently as she untied the ropes on Marcia's wrists. She was sobbing too hard to even speak. "Are you hurt?" Wendy said sharply as she searched for any sign of bleeding or injury.

"No," Marcia gulped out. "I'm okay, I'm okay," she said quickly.

"Who did this to you?" Wendy asked with growing concern.

"I don't know," Marcia gasped out. "This man in a mask showed up at my house. He told me I had to come with him, to get him into Camilla's office. I tried telling him I didn't have a key, but he just pried the door open. He wanted me to get into Camilla's computer. But I told him I don't have the password to her computer, only her assistants do. I only have a password to my computer. He started tearing the place up thinking he could find the password stored somewhere."

"Did he?" Wendy glanced around the room and noticed that Camilla's computer was missing.

"No, I don't think so. He finally just took the computer and left me here," Marcia began to cry again.

"You never saw his face?" Wendy asked, and looked directly into Marcia's eyes.

"No, I didn't," she insisted.

"What about his voice?" Wendy asked hopefully. "Did you notice anything about his voice."

"He just growled at me, and whispered, I couldn't really understand him half the time," she frowned. "I'm so sorry."

"It's okay," Wendy said and hugged Marcia gently. "I'm going to get the police and an ambulance here," she started to dial the police, but at the last minute decided to dial Brian instead.

"I just arrived at Camilla's office and found Marcia, her receptionist, tied up and the office ransacked. Someone abducted Marcia from her house and brought her here, she's okay, but she's shaken up," she said swiftly right after he answered.

"Wow, wait, what?" Brian sputtered into the phone. "Didn't I tell you to call me if..."

"I'm calling you now, aren't I?" Wendy pointed out with a grim tone in her voice. "I haven't called the police yet."

"Don't," Brian said with some urgency. "I'll call them. You need to get out of there."

"I can't leave Marcia alone," Wendy argued, as the woman was still trembling in her arms.

"I'll be there in two minutes, don't move. If the police show up, don't say a word," he instructed sternly before hanging up the phone.

The very idea of the police arriving and finding Wendy in the middle of such a mess was terrifying to her. She could only think it would make her look more guilty. As she waited for Brian to arrive and comforted Marcia the best she could, her mind shifted to the woman she had expected to meet.

"Wait, Marcia, did you tell this man that Camilla's assistants would know how to get into her computer?" Wendy asked with anxiety growing in her voice.

"I did," she sniffled and nodded. "It's the truth. Camilla never trusted me with her computer. She only trusted you."

"But what about Veronica?" Wendy asked in a whisper. "Did she give the password to Veronica?"

"I think so," Marcia shook her head. "I don't know for sure."

Wendy looked down at her phone to see that Veronica still hadn't texted her back. She dialed Veronica's number, but after four rings her voicemail picked up.

"Veronica, it's Wendy, please give me a call as soon as you get this," Wendy said as she waved a hand to Brian who was just walking in. He stared around at the destruction wide-eyed and then rushed over to check on Marcia. As Wendy hung up the phone she frowned.

"I think Veronica might be in danger," she said swiftly. "Will you stay here with Marcia until the police get here?"

"Where are you going?" Brian asked as he looked up at her, his hazel eyes shadowed with concern. "If Veronica is in danger we need to tell the police."

"There may not be time for that," Wendy called over her shoulder as she hurried back down the hallway. "I will call you!" she hollered just as his lips parted to make the request.

She hopped into her car and began driving in the direction of the hotel that she knew Veronica was staying in. She could only hope that she would get there in time. As she drove, the roads were packed with tourist traffic. Her phone began to ring shrilly. She didn't even look at the caller ID before she picked it up.

"Brian, I said I would call," she said with annoyance.

"Wendy, it's me John," John's voice carried through the phone full of stress. "I know that there's a lot going on, but I really need you to talk to Brenda. She's starting to freak out about the reception, and the entrée, and..."

"John, it's okay," Wendy said trying to calm him. "There isn't anything that we can do about the entrée now. I will talk with Brenda about whatever is upsetting her, but the most important thing is that you stay calm, and you let her know that you are with her and supporting her."

"But she's locked herself in our room and won't come out," John said desperately. "Can you please come and talk to her?"

"I..." Wendy hesitated. She knew how important the wedding was to John and Brenda, it was important to her, too, but she was very concerned about Veronica's safety. "Give me an hour, okay John?" she said quickly. "If you don't hear from me by then, go to the store and buy a huge bouquet of flowers and rent her favorite movie. She's not upset with you, she's just feeling overwhelmed."

"Okay," John sighed. "I'll do that. Thanks, Wendy."

"I'll be there soon," Wendy promised him before she hung up the phone. She dialed Veronica again. It rang several times and just as she was expecting it to go to voicemail, the line picked up. There was a prolonged silence.

"Veronica?" Wendy asked nervously.

"No," a voice with a thick accent replied.

"Who is this?" Wendy demanded though she suspected that she already knew.

"Meet me at 3-A," he requested in a calm but confident tone. "Then we can discuss who I am."

"Giuseppe?" Wendy asked as she slowed her car down and pulled it onto the side of the road. "Where's Veronica? Is she with you?" she asked urgently.

"Don't you worry about Veronica, Wendy," he chuckled into the phone. "We reached a mutual understanding. Now, you and I need to have a conversation of our own. Don't even think about bringing any police or anyone else for that matter, or Veronica might never have the chance to drink another glass of wine."

He hung up the phone before Wendy could say another word. She stared down at the phone before setting it down on the passenger seat. She knew she should call for help, the police or at least Brian, but the very idea that Veronica's life might be hanging in the balance left her completely petrified. Her heart began to beat faster. She wondered what would happen if she followed Giuseppe's instructions. Would he be waiting there for her? She closed her eyes briefly as she recalled Marcia's words that only Camilla's assistants would know how to access her computer. Was he after her, too?

Wendy's hands shook as she put them back on the wheel. Her foot felt numb as she stepped down on the gas and pulled back out onto the road. She wasn't sure how she got from that point to the resort, but she soon found herself in the parking lot. She drew a deep breath and picked up her phone. As she made her way slowly across the parking lot, she could see that the conference area of the resort was dark. It was already closed for the day. Wendy knew that there would not be anyone around to help her if she got herself into trouble. She played with her phone for a moment, passing it back and forth between her hands. She was certain that if she texted Brian, he would come right away which might put Veronica's life at risk.

She tucked her phone into her pocket and walked up to the door. When she turned the knob it opened easily. Either someone had forgotten to lock it, or someone had left it open on purpose. She made her way through the dimly lit hallways to conference room 3-A. It was not blocked off with yellow tape as she had hoped it might be. She knew that Brian was supposed to be checking into it earlier, but she could only guess that nothing had come of it, because it didn't look as if any police had combed over it. She peered through the rectangular glass window beside the door. The room was dark, and she couldn't see anyone else inside.

Wendy's heart thumped heavily as she remembered the fear she had seen in Marcia's eyes. Giuseppe was ruthless. Slowly she opened the door to the conference room. She inched her way inside. It was dark in the back of the conference room. The light that filtered through the windows towards the front didn't make it all the way to the rear. When Wendy tried to see through the shadows, she only succeeded in causing her vision to get blurry. She didn't have to see to know that someone was there. Softly, she heard the rustle of the carpet beneath the sole of a shoe. Her heart pounded heavily and hard against her chest as she froze where she stood. She knew that she should move, or call out, but she simply couldn't. The fear that was coursing through her made her stand perfectly still. This would have been great if she was in the woods with a bear, but instead, she was in the dark with a man she thought was a murderer.

"You shouldn't have gotten in the middle of my business," he said without moving again. She couldn't quite tell where he was. His voice seemed a little distorted.

"I'm not here to cause any trouble, I'm just here to get Veronica," Wendy said in what she expected to be a brave voice. However, when she heard her own voice, it did not sound brave at all, it sounded more than a little terrified.

"Veronica?" the man laughed and even his laughter sounded incredibly cruel. "Isn't that sweet, you think you're some kind of hero."

"No, I don't," Wendy said quickly and honestly. "Listen, this doesn't have to be a big deal, just tell me where she is, and we'll both be on our way."

When he took a step closer to her, Wendy felt a strong shiver course along her spine. She almost couldn't breathe when his rich brown eyes met hers through the remaining shadows.

"I'm afraid I can't do that, Wendy," he said in a mocking whisper that made her certain he was going to enjoy whatever he decided to do to her.

"Please," Wendy murmured. She didn't feel the need to put on a tough act when Veronica's, and now her own life, was on the line. "No one has to know about your past. We all have pasts. As far as I'm concerned, you just haven't been happy in marriage, just unfortunate matches. You didn't do anything wrong," Wendy tried her best to sound convincing.

"Right," he nodded a little. "So, I should be able to trust you, not to tell any of my secrets, hmm?" his thick accent coursed over Wendy's nerves like nails on a chalkboard. To think she had once been enamored by it, when she had first met him, during the preparation for his first marriage when he used Camilla's company. She had been so distracted by the melodic rhythm of his voice that she hadn't paid attention to his wandering eyes.

"Exactly," Wendy replied, though she could sense that he was not exactly agreeing with her. "So, just tell me where Veronica is, please," she added and held his gaze directly.

"I'm afraid I can't do that," he replied, in a voice so low that Wendy barely heard it.

"Why not?" Wendy asked, her heart pounding desperately. The more she spoke to this man the more dangerous he seemed to her.

"Because, Veronica is already gone," he replied. His words hung in the air before Wendy. Her stomach clenched and her chest tightened. Had he killed Veronica to keep her silent, too?

Chapter Eight

"Did you kill her?" Wendy asked her teeth chattering.

"Did I kill her?" he replied and she felt his hands encircle her wrists. "No, I didn't kill her," he laughed a little and pulled Wendy towards an empty chair.

"Wait, no," Wendy tried to pull away from him but his grip was strong. She was beginning to panic even more. "No, just let me go!" she demanded.

"I would," Giuseppe replied with a snort. "I really would, if I thought that you were anything like Veronica. But you're not. Veronica took the money, and happily. After explaining to her that I had to kill Camilla because she wanted too much money from me to keep quiet she even told me that she didn't hold anything against me for killing her. She's one cold lady," he laughed again, as he forced Wendy down into the chair. "That's why I don't have to worry about her. But you," he frowned as he looked directly at Wendy. "You would never let it go, would you?"

Wendy stared up at him with fear in her eyes, she didn't know how to answer the question. She could lie and say she would, but she knew that he wouldn't believe her.

"I don't want any money," Wendy said quickly. "I just want you to let me go. That's all."

"And you'll let me go on to steal every dime from my new wife?" he inquired with mirth in his voice. Wendy started to nod, but the pain in her expression must have given her away. "No, you just can't, can you?" he asked as he began tying a rope around her wrists, fastening her to the arms of the chair she was sitting in. "True love is too important to you, to let a man like me go free."

"It's fine," Wendy lied as she looked up at him pleadingly. "It's your life, your business. I won't do anything to interfere..."

The sharp way he tightened the rope on her wrists silenced her. She knew as she stared at him with growing anticipation of her own demise, that he was not going to believe anything she said.

"You're not going to survive this, you know

that, Wendy?" he asked with an almost kind smile as he looked into her eyes. "You know when I offed Camilla I didn't mind too much. She's always been a royal pain. But you," he sighed as he traced his fingertips along her cheek. "You, I didn't expect to have to kill. It's not that I think you deserve to die, but there's just no other way."

"I'm the one that found out the truth about you," Wendy challenged and glared at him directly in his eyes. Now that she knew he wasn't going to let her go, she was getting angry. "I'm the one that told Camilla about you."

"Then I guess you're just as guilty as me," he chuckled as he stood up and turned towards the table where his gun was stowed. "If you hadn't been so interfering, Camilla would still be alive, and you and I wouldn't be having this difficult conversation," he explained as he turned back to her. "But then, I guess just like Camilla's death, yours won't be much of a tragedy. No husband, no kids, right?" he smirked a little as he held the gun in his hand, just close enough to Wendy's face for her to see it.

"There's nothing I can do to stop you,"

Wendy said with a grim frown as she waited for the inevitable. "It wouldn't matter if I had a husband or children, and you know it."

"You're right, it wouldn't," he admitted as he released the safety on the weapon. "Any last words?" he suggested.

Wendy gritted her teeth. She didn't want to cry. She didn't want to give him the satisfaction of seeing her tears as he pulled the trigger.

"You're a murderer," she hissed as she stared at him.

"You're right, I am, and a cheat, and a blackmailer, and just an all round bad guy," he shrugged a little. "I'm just so good at it. But the best part of all of this is that everyone is going to think that you're the murderer, not me. Your guilt got the best of you, and you committed suicide to atone for your terrible act."

"No one will believe that," Wendy said quickly.

"Oh, sure they will," he chuckled. "Because I know how to make it look like a suicide."

"If it was a real suicide, then I would be back at the scene of the crime. The place where I killed

Camilla," she nearly choked on those words.

"Huh," Giuseppe mumbled and glanced over his shoulder before looking back at her. "That's really not a bad idea."

He stared at her for a long moment in the chair she was tied to. She could tell that he was considering her words.

"Yeah, it would look a little suspicious for you to kill yourself in here, I guess," he shrugged mildly and then reached for her arm. He held onto it tightly while he untied the rope from around the chair.

"Get up!" he instructed her with a sharp tone and gave her arm a firm jerk.

"Okay, okay," Wendy said, feeling very flustered as she nearly lost her balance when he pulled her up.

"Start walking," he said and poked the gun hard into her back. Wendy shuddered at the feeling of the barrel pushing against her shirt. To her there was nothing more powerful than a gun. She reluctantly stepped out of the conference room. With each step she hoped that someone would notice her, a member of the staff would see her and offer help. But it was very late, and the conference rooms of the hotel were all locked up and already cleaned. He pushed her towards a side door that led out of the main lobby and onto the beach. Even the lobby was completely vacant.

When Wendy stepped out onto the beach she could feel grains of sand slipping into her sandals. The sensation was normally soothing for her, but now she was terrified. The closer she got to the edge of the crashing waves, the more certain she was that this would be her last walk on the beach.

***

Wendy stumbled further along on the beach. Her legs were weak with fear. She could barely stand up straight. But Giuseppe helped her with that by keeping a firm grip on her arm and holding her steady. The entire time she could feel the firm muzzle of the gun shoved into her lower back. She knew one wrong move could mean the end of her life. She wasn't ready for that yet. She hadn't found her great love, as she always had expected to. She hadn't had the chance to grow her business into a success. There was so much she still wanted to experience and accomplish. In particular, the thought that came to mind, was the memory of Brian's arms around her. That was something she was certain she wanted to experience again, no matter where it led. The beach was deserted. She knew if she screamed someone might hear her, but by the time they came to help, the trigger would be pulled.

"Please, just let me go," she said as she tried to wriggle out of his grasp.

"We talked about this Wendy, that can't happen," he warned her. "Just think, you're giving your life to ensure that a marriage will last," he laughed a little. "At least until she signs all of her financial information and holdings over to me, as well as that sweet little house in Mexico."

"Don't you ever get tired of stealing and killing?" Wendy asked, though she knew the question was a little absurd. "Don't you ever wish that you could find true love, someone who you wouldn't have to trick into being with you?"

"Oh, I don't trick them," Giuseppe breathed

beside her ear. "They hear my accent, they see my big brown eyes, they lap up every promise I make them. I don't trick them at all. I can't help that they want what I offer them. They're so love-starved and desperate for affection that they don't think their decisions through. Is that my fault?" he asked.

Wendy was feeling very sick to her stomach. She knew that this man could not be reasoned with. She heard the crash of the waves against the sand. She heard the slow retreat of them pulling back.

"Please, can I take my shoes off?" she asked, her voice trembling.

"Your shoes?" he asked and looked at her strangely.

"Please," Wendy said as she glanced up at the stars that littered the sky. "I like to feel the sand beneath my feet. It's just one thing I'm asking for."

He hesitated as if he suspected that she might be tricking him. She wasn't. She wanted to feel the sand beneath her feet. But she was also stalling. She hoped that someone somehow would suddenly walk out onto the beach, or perhaps a boat would see her from afar. She had never been in such a dire situation, but it was hard for her to believe that these were the last moments of her life.

"Okay," he reluctantly agreed. "But slide them off easy."

"Okay," she replied and used the toe of one sandal to push the other one off. Then she knocked the second sandal off with her bare toes. Once her feet sank into the sand she breathed a sigh of relief. It was as if everything abruptly shifted, and despite her terror, she found some sense of peace.

She saw the gun pointed at her and then heard the safety catch release. She closed her eyes and drew a long slow breath of the warm salty air. Then she heard it, the loud explosion of a bullet leaving its chamber. She hadn't expected to hear it. She thought it would be so fast that she would never know it happened. She braced herself, expecting to experience pain beyond her imagination. But she didn't. Instead she felt something else. A heavy body falling against hers. Wendy was so shocked that she didn't even think to move out of the way. Giuseppe collapsed on her and knocked her into the water. She wriggled in an attempt to get free, still confused about what had just happened. Then she saw it, the flashing lights. There were police cars on the beach. She hadn't even noticed them arrive. There was shouting as she felt the water lapping against her face, washing the tears away that she hadn't even realized were falling.

Someone lifted Giuseppe off her and she heard him groan in protest. He was still alive, but for how long she had no idea. The gunshot she had heard must have been directed at him. But by whom?

Strong arms pulled her up out of the water. She drew in a heavy breath and was about to cry out when those arms wrapped around her, and their warmth silenced her fear. She felt her heart flutter in her chest, not from fear, but from familiarity. She looked up into Brian's eyes, which were filled with concern.

"Did he hurt you?" he asked as he gazed at her intently. She had never seen his hazel gaze so dark.

"No," she managed to whisper. "I'm okay."

"Wendy," he sighed and held her closer. "You're okay," he repeated with relief in his voice.

"We're going to need a statement," Officer Polson said from a few feet away. She looked over at him as she reluctantly pulled out of Brian's arms.

"You want a statement?" Wendy asked.

"Yes," Polson nodded as he holstered his weapon. Wendy became vaguely aware that he must have been the one who had shot Giuseppe and ultimately saved her life.

"I'm innocent," she said and swallowed thickly. "Just like I told you three days ago."

Polson frowned but offered her a slight nod. "You can take a few moments, then we'll have some questions for you."

As Polson walked away, Wendy turned back to Brian.

"How did you know?" she asked him. "I know it wasn't Polson that figured all of this out."

"It wasn't me either," he admitted with a touch of guilt. "I was making calls to all of the contacts I found. I decided to call Veronica again. When I told her we were investigating Giuseppe, she admitted that she had taken a bribe from him. She told me how Giuseppe had called her to the same conference room with the intention to kill her. When I couldn't reach you, I knew," he sighed and shook his head. "It never should have happened this way. I'm sorry you went through all of that."

"I'm not," Wendy said with a hint of bravery in her voice. "Camilla needed someone to solve her problem one last time. Giuseppe is a truly terrible man."

"Yes, he is," Brian agreed. "And now he won't hurt anyone ever again. Do you want me to drive you home?" he offered.

"Yes, please," Wendy said. "Right after I finish with Polson."

***

Polson went easy on Wendy with his questions. When he was finished, she looked at him with a slight smile. "It was you, wasn't it?"

124

she asked as she studied him.

"What do you mean?" he asked.

"You saved me," she said calmly.

"Well, technically it was Brian, he's the one that tipped us off," he said with a mild shrug.

"But you're the one who pulled the trigger," Wendy pointed out. "Thank you."

"Just doing my job," he said sternly and then met her eyes. "Just like I said before. It was nothing personal."

"Well, don't take this personally," Wendy said as she looked at him. "But I hope we never meet again."

"Agreed," Polson nodded and offered his hand. She took it and gave it a quick, firm shake. Then she walked back across the sand to Brian who was waiting for her near the parking lot.

"Are you sure you're okay?" Brian asked as he looked her over from head to toe. "Your shoes..." he started to say.

"I don't want them," Wendy said quickly. "I don't ever want to put those shoes back on."

"Okay," Brian nodded slowly and reached up

to brush back a strawberry blonde curl that had fallen in Wendy's face. "Let me get you home."

As Brian drove towards her condo, Wendy felt her heart sink. She couldn't bring herself to speak. So much had unfolded in so little time. But the only thing truly on her mind was Brian's touch, which he seemed to be cautious about offering her. She knew that once he dropped her off she would probably never see him again. His job was done. When she made some money, she would mail him a check. That would be that. Anything more that she thought might be happening, was all in her imagination.

Wendy's cell phone began to ring. Brian glanced over at her as she answered the phone.

"Hi John," she said in an attempt to be cheerful. "Is Brenda still locked in her room?"

"No, you were right, she's okay now," John said with a sigh. "I just wanted to thank you and let you know that you don't need to come over tonight."

"Oh good," Wendy said with relief. She didn't think she could make it without a little rest first. "I will see you first thing in the morning then."

"Okay," John said quickly. "See you then."

As Wendy hung up the phone she felt Brian's eyes still on her. He had already pulled into the parking lot of her condo.

"Everything okay?" he asked as he pulled into a parking space.

"Sounds like it," Wendy laughed a little. "Just pre-wedding nerves."

"Are you really going to go tomorrow?" he asked with a furrowed brow. "Don't you think you've earned a day off?"

"Well, that's the best part about doing something that you love," Wendy explained. "It never feels like work, it always feels like a privilege."

"That's a good point," he said quietly and glanced away. "It was a privilege to work with you, Wendy," he said.

"Thank you for everything you did to help me," she replied. "I never would have made it through this without you."

"Oh, I tend to doubt that," he chuckled as he looked over at her again. "You seem very capable of taking care of yourself."

"Maybe," she replied with a hint of sadness in her voice. "I guess this is it," she said as she opened her car door.

"Wendy, if you ever need anything, just call me," he said swiftly as he reached for her hand. When he took her hand she felt that same wave rush upward through her.

"Anything?" she asked as she looked back at him with warmth in her eyes.

"Anything," he nodded, still holding firmly to her hand.

"I could use a date for the wedding," she said with a playful smile.

"Uh, well," Brian flushed at that. Wendy immediately regretted asking. She was sure that any connection between them had all been in her head. "I don't usually do weddings," he continued awkwardly.

"Oh sure, I'm sorry, I shouldn't have asked," she said and tugged her hand free of his.

"No, wait," he looked up at her and smiled. "Maybe it's time I saw one through your eyes. I'll meet you there?"

"At noon," she said with a smile.

As Wendy walked barefoot into her condo, she didn't notice the cold of the floor beneath her feet, because she was fairly certain she was walking on air.

Chapter Nine

Wendy woke up in time to see the sunrise the next morning. There was something poetic about watching the colors change in the sky, as she had thought she might never see them again. The weather was perfect for the wedding. Brenda was already calling her as she drove to the resort.

"I'm almost there, Brenda," Wendy said cheerfully.

"But I just heard about everything that happened on the beach last night. Is it true? Wendy, were you involved?" Brenda asked anxiously.

"We can talk about all of that after you get back from your honeymoon," Wendy said quickly. "The important thing is that I am fine, and it's your wedding day!"

Brenda squealed with excitement. "I absolutely have to be the luckiest woman on earth!" she announced.

Wendy smiled. That was exactly how she wanted Brenda to feel. When she pulled into the parking lot of the resort she could see that the archway was already being constructed out on the sand. The white chairs were being lined up, and there was already a golden runner stretched across the sand for Brenda to walk across.

There were musicians setting up, and the catering vans were arriving. Brenda had chosen a noon wedding so they would have all afternoon to celebrate. Wendy thought it was a wonderful idea. As she walked into the resort she smiled at a few of Brenda's bridesmaids, who were attending to the groomsmen. Something about weddings made it impossible for a man to tie a tie.

"Brenda?" Wendy called out as she stepped into the room that she was using to get ready in.

Brenda turned around to face Wendy. She could not have looked more like a princess. She was wearing a traditional white gown with a very fluffy full skirt, and a plain silver tiara to hold her veil in place. She smiled at Wendy as Wendy gasped softly in admiration.

"Oh Brenda, you look so beautiful," Wendy said and offered her a very gentle hug.

"Thanks to you I'm rested, I'm not stressed, and I feel beautiful," Brenda said as she hugged her back. "You're a real lifesaver, Wendy."

Wendy grinned a little at that. She hoped that Brenda would never be faced with a real life or death situation like Wendy had the night before. It was nice to be called a lifesaver, but she had been saved by some real heroes last night.

"Are you ready?" Wendy asked as she looked Brenda over.

"A little too early," Brenda admitted with a guilty smile. "I just couldn't resist putting it on."

"Just leave it on," Wendy insisted. "The make-up can be done with a cape around you. Your hair is going to be wonderful."

As the two chatted about the wedding, Wendy felt the last traces of fear from the night before leaving her. She was in her element again, planning the perfect day for yet another amazing bride.

"I'm going to go check on everything," she said as the make-up artist arrived to work on Brenda.

"Okay," Brenda smiled. "Thanks again."

Wendy walked out to the beach to find that the decorations were being put in place. She checked on the roses which were beautiful and just the right shade of pink. Everything was coming together nicely. It was hard to believe that just a few miles down the beach Wendy had been facing such terror the night before. Just as a wave of fear washed over her she turned to find Brian standing at the edge of the sand. He had his shoes off, and his bare toes sunk deep.

"Hi, Brian," Wendy said as she walked up to him.

"Hi," he replied shyly. Now that Wendy wasn't his client, his confidence level seemed to have been knocked down a notch. He was dressed in a black suit with an off-white button down shirt. His dark hair was combed carefully, and his hazel eyes were drinking in the sight of her.

"You look lovely," she said before realizing how silly that might sound to a man.

"Uh, thank you," Brian blushed and smiled. "So do you."

Wendy grinned as she knew that her simple

summer sundress was pretty but nothing exquisite. She had to wear something she could be comfortable in, and get dirty in if necessary. She never knew what might happen at a wedding.

She and Brian shared a quick coffee while Wendy supervised the last minute issues of the wedding. Soon the guests had arrived and everyone was seated on the beach. Wendy and Brian sat towards the back. Brian was shifting a little uncomfortably. Wendy pretended not to notice, but she was having to hold back her laughter. She could see that he really was not comfortable at weddings. Then the music started playing. Wendy opened her purse and pulled out a packet of tissues.

"What's wrong?" Brian asked in a whisper.

"Oh, I always cry at weddings," Wendy said with a smile. "If they're done right, that is," she winked at him. He looked a little confused at why she would be so emotional, but she ignored it. The bride walking down the aisle was her favorite part. The music swelled, and Brenda began walking down the aisle towards John. John looked so proud, and eager as he watched her approach. Brenda was gazing lovingly in his direction. Despite picking out all the decorations, all the special details that seemed so important at the time, neither John or Brenda were looking at any of them. They couldn't take their eyes off each other.

Wendy wiped lightly at a tear that slid down her cheek. She sniffled as Brenda reached John. Just as the ceremony was about to begin, she felt that sensation of a wave again as Brian's hand brushed over hers. She glanced in his direction and could see a slight smile on his face.

Wendy grinned to herself as she was sure that despite all that had gone wrong, Brenda and John's wedding was one thing that had gone perfectly right.

The End

More Cozy Mysteries by Cindy Bell

Dune House Cozy Mystery Series

Seaside Secrets

Heavenly Highland Inn Cozy Mystery Series

Murdering the Roses

Dead in the Daisies

Killing the Carnations

Drowning the Daffodils

Suffocating the Sunflowers

Bekki the Beautician Cozy Mystery Series

Hairspray and Homicide

A Dyed Blonde and a Dead Body

Mascara and Murder

Pageant and Poison

Conditioner and a Corpse

Mistletoe, Makeup and Murder

Hairpin, Hair Dryer and Homicide

Blush, a Bride and a Body

Shampoo and a Stiff

Cosmetics, a Cruise and a Killer